For me, today is gonna be busy. I've gotta make a quick run over to Jenny's this afternoon in order for us to exchange gifts, and then I've gotta get back here in time for dinner. On Christmas Eve we usually eat right at six pm, and then we have this little family-type traditional thing that we do. We all go into our living room right after dinner, fire up the fireplace, and then sip on coffee or eggnog together. That's pretty nice, ain't it?

There's also the slight chance that if we beg, plead, or just plain get on Mama's nerves enough that she might let us open one Christmas gift. Underline the word "might." We'll be really lucky if that happens, though, because Ed Jr. and my mom believe in opening gifts on Christmas morning only. Mama says we do that to be sure we celebrate Jesus' birthday when we're supposed to. Ed Jr. says that we open them then so that he doesn't have to listen to any pissing and moaning about us not having any gifts left to open. He adds that if anyone has a right to a peaceful Christmas, it's him, as he has to cut down and put up the tree, deal with Mama's relatives, and pay the tab for our entire Christmas. Not to mention the fact that he's a Korean veteran. You've got to admit his logic is not bad, and at least it's pretty original.

Champagne Books Presents

ChristmaSin'

A Juliette Christmas Epistle

By

Ed Williams

This is a work of fiction. The characters, incidents and dialogues in this book are of the author's imagination and are not to be construed as real. Any resemblance to actual events or persons, living or dead, is completely coincidental.

Champagne Books
www.champagnebooks.com

ISBN 978-1-926681-59-7
November 2009
Cover Art © Trisha FitzGerald
Produced in Canada

Champagne Books
#35069-4604 37 ST SW
Calgary, AB T3E 7C7
Canada

Champagne

Dedication

For Miss Lily..

Dr. B, I'm sorry you're not in this one but you're still the Elvis of dentists!

[illegible]

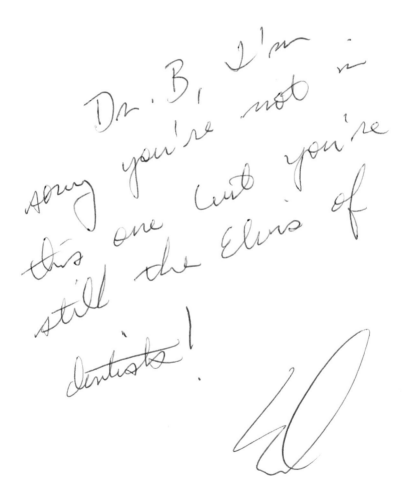

Prologue

Christmas has to be the most popular holiday there is. The meaning of the season, combined with its rampant commercialism, ensures its place as the holiday that touches our hearts (and wallets) the most. Who doesn't reflect warmly on the circumstances surrounding the birth of Christ, and who doesn't also greatly enjoy receiving the bounty of gifts that accompanies this festive season? It's a season that appeals to our best, and sometimes, worst instincts at the same time.

I love Christmas. Well, let me restate that and be a tad more honest. I love the meaning behind the season, yet I hate its commercial aspects as they can hinder our understanding of the holiday. It's very important that everyone understands that Christ loved us and was put here so that we might have a chance at true redemption of our sins. By God, if anyone ever needed a chance at redeeming sins it's me, and I'm glad that I have a shot at it before I proceed onwards to that great bream hole in the sky.

All that having been said, I want to take a stab at writing about a typical Juliette Christmas from years ago. Juliette, like most rural Georgia towns, had its own particular Christmas customs and activities, and more stories surrounding them than I will ever be able to remember here.

Even so, I'm going to take some true Christmas events that occurred over past years in Juliette, blend them together with a little creative license, and hopefully end up with a Juliette Christmas story that is both representative of its era and one that you'll enjoy reading. I can hardly wait to write it—it gives me a chance to enjoy the holiday yet one more time with Ed Sr., Miss Lily, Calhoun, my mom, and others very dear to me who were tremendously important parts of the Christmases of my youth. I love my family more than I can say, and writing this book makes them live again, one more precious time.

So, get ready for my first (and probably only) attempt at a novel, a novel that is heartfelt, somewhat true, and one I hope will make you laugh, reflect, and have another reason to appreciate this grand holiday for what it is—the King of all Holidays honoring the King of all Kings.

One

It's October of 1972, and the bitter cold slippin' into Juliette tells me that this may be a very different season from those past…

Something unusual is definitely in the air. Weather-wise alone, Juliette normally would be enjoying sixty to seventy degree days, and thirty to forty degree nights during this time of the year. As it is, our daytime temps are around thirty-five to forty degrees, and the nights are just witch-tit cold—like twenty to twenty-five degrees, and have even been colder than that a couple of times, if you can believe it.

Personally, Brother and I don't mind the cold too much, except for the fact that we have to wear these damned long-sleeved flannel shirts on top of our regular t-shirts. Big, thick flannel shirts, and they carry all sorts of smells with them. I don't know what it is about flannel, but if you're standing by a fire, a flannel shirt will smell like smoke. If you hug a lady wearing perfume, you might as well have dabbed on some yourself. And don't even get me started about farts—one time I was wearing a flannel shirt, stood next to someone that major farted, and got accused of breaking wind by my mom later on in the day. I tried telling her that I wasn't guilty, but she told me the odor was dank and that I should be ashamed of lying to her about it. So I hate these damned flannel shirts.

Fortunately, it turns out that Brother hates flannel shirts, too, so we've decided today that we're going to wrestle out in the grass. If we do that we figure we'll get grass stains all over these damned shirts, and it'll force Mama to give us something else to wear. Anything would beat these shirts, even if we have to wear pajama tops, t-shirts, or whatever. I'd even live with wearing a girl's t-shirt in this cold, as long as someone doesn't drive up unexpectedly to the house and see me wearing it. Anything beats flannel.

Well, before we can even begin to put a hurtin' on these shirts, we have to eat breakfast. This morning's fare is coffee and raisin bran, and Brother and I are eating it like it is our last supper. Mama is pretty cool regarding coffee. We're actually allowed to drink it any way we want it which, for me, is with plenty of cream and sugar mixed in. Brother is kinda the king of cool coffee drinkin', though. He actually drinks his black sometimes, and won't even make faces when he slurps it down. He can be really major like that.

Ed Jr. comes in to eat breakfast, and before he even chugs down one sip of coffee he starts heavy cussin' one of the county commissioners in Forsyth for voting to pave some road over in Bolingbroke. Personally, I don't see what the big deal is. I mean, who gives a shit about one more or less paved road over in Bolingbroke? Well, it's now obvious as hell that Ed Jr. does. He says that one particular county commissioner is behind it, and that the reason why is that he's married and fooling around with a baggy old married lady over in Smarr. One with frizzed up red hair and navel level boobs, if you want the level facts about it. And the reason why he wants this road paved? Per Ed Jr., "…so that when he screws her in the back seat of his car over there each and every Friday night, it won't have dust and mud caked all over it when he slips back over to Smarr." For me, it makes as much sense as most of the other stuff our local politicians do, but for some reason it's making Ed Jr. madder than hell. Brother and I quickly figure out that this is one of those conversations that Ed Jr. has best with himself, so we both figure that quickly eating our raisin bran and taking long looks out the back window is the smartest thing for us to do. And that's exactly what happens.

Ed Jr. eats his salmon and grits pretty quickly, as he has

to go into work early this morning for some kind of safety class or something. My mom has let us know that she has a ton of housework to do, and if Brother and I are inside it means that we will be drafted to do God only knows what. You know, mothers don't seem to mind asking you to do anything when it comes to working inside a house. You might scrub a toilet, beat rugs, or even have to scrape some nail polish off a countertop. I had to do that one time, and it would've been just as much fun to take deep breaths around someone who has diarrhea. I remember Mama gave me this tiny little piece of sandpaper to scrape it off with, but you couldn't have made it come up from there with an atomic bomb. The worse thing was that it was hard to even see where the nail polish was—it was clear and really just sort of blended into the counter. I wouldn't have even screwed with it, but Mama can be just as hardheaded as the old man, if not more so. So there was nothing to do but try to scrape up that damned polish. I didn't get much of it off, but I did a damn good job of rounding down the ends of some of my fingertips. Good deeds sometimes suck for the doer, you know.

Brother and I both look at each other, nod, and outside we go. We go out through our garage and into the front yard quicker than a preacher sits down for dinner. The only thing is, once we get out there we have to figure out real quick-like what it is we're going to do, or else we'll be inside dealing with mildewed tub grout or Drano for most of the day. And when I begin thinking about the joys of putting out flypaper for a full day, Brother comes up with the idea of going off into the cow pasture to play a game of "Commando." Since I haven't come up with anything better, it sounds like a true winner, so off we go like two-legged cows towards their homeland.

I love running, but I should've learned by now not to go into a full-assed run straight into our pasture. There are tons of briars everywhere, and even if you avoid all of them, there are the ten thousand or so spider webs that are built between all these bushes and vines. Spiders are definitely a-screwin' down here in Juliette. But, I guess with all things considered, gettin' pocked up by a few briars and pullin' a few spider webs off our heads aren't such a bad trade-off when you consider what else we could be doin'. In the end, we really don't suffer all that badly from our run, and we soon find ourselves next to a series of huge red clay ditches that are sort of like a miniature version of Tallulah Gorge. This particular one that we are standing close to has to be at least a good five or six feet deep. As we stand here hassling like horny puppies, Brother runs through the rules of "Commando."

"First, this round of Commando is gonna be played only in these red mud ditches. No goin' off in the woods or anything, okay?"

I nod agreement.

"Now, when we begin, we walk in opposite directions 'til we reach the end of this red mud pit, okay?"

"Okay."

"Next, you're allowed to carry two chunks of clay on you. One big one in your hand, and one small one in your pocket. And, as near as you can tell, the chunks have to be all clay, one hundred percent, no rocks in 'em or anything."

"Just two?" I ask. "Damn, what if you miss with both of 'em?"

Brother gives me a look like he is some kinda religious scholar and says, "Well, then you get ready to die an honorable death, sort of like the Japanese did in World War II. Look at it sort of like a Georgia suicide mission."

"Okay, I can go with that."

Brother continues, "The first one to score a direct hit on the other's clothes wins the game. And, if you miss with both chunks, all bets are off, and the first person who can pick up a chunk and nail the other one wins." Brother smiles right after he says this.

I say, "I like that, sort of sudden death like."

"And one more thing," he adds. "This is for all the marbles."

"All the marbles? What does that mean?"

"Edward, the loser of this war has to let Mama see them

in their clothes afterwards. No early baths or sneaking around or anything. She has to see you all slicked over with mud, and you have to listen to everything she says and do anything that she tells you to do."

I flinch a little. "Damn, ain't that a tad fierce? That could be a whole lot of shit for one person to have to take."

"War's hell," he responds.

Against all known logic I reply, "Okay, I agree. Let's do it."

Brother and I start walking away from each other. Soon as we get out of each other's eyesight, I figure that I've gotta find some chunks of clay fast. Brother can throw the living hell out of anything, and he's at his best with a chunk of clay, and on top of that, his accuracy is good. If I spend very much time looking for clay, chances are I'll be receiving some when it explodes up against my face. So, I immediately start looking around in some places that are on the fringes of this little clay pit I find myself in. The first little gully or two doesn't turn up much, but then things get better. I find one section of clay where there are lots of cracks running all through it, on account of how the sun baked it. Some of the cracks are so big that you could stick your foot down in 'em and wiggle it around. With a set up like that, all I have to do is reach down and pull a few chunks out. Of the ones that I get, one is sort of softball-sized and easy to throw. Another is almost identically shaped like one of those tiny little rubber footballs that you get from some of these high pocket insurance agents. That one goes right into my pocket, and from that, it's now time to sneak up on Brother and whunk his ass into oblivion with my two red grenades.

I've gotta think up a good strategy now and quick, 'cause sittin' still in this game means a whupped ass. So I think real hard for a good half a minute or so, and decide that I'll sneak right up the middle of one of these long ditches, go really, really slow as I do it, and listen really, really hard. Listening is the most crucial part of the stalk. If I go slow and listen hard, Brother has to make some kind of racket. He could step on a stick or step on some clay that's too dry and cause it to crack off the side of the ditch and tumble down. Then, if I hear it, I'll know exactly where he is. And when I know, I can glide over there, cock my arm, and laugh when I put a red chunk right between his beady little eyes.

So I commence carrying it out. I go really, really slow, slower than a sleepy Florida porch dog. It's hell on my knees, 'cause I'm squatted down low, easing my way through this long ass ditch. You know, considering it's just some old red clay here in Georgia, this is really a deep damn ditch. The sides are wide enough so that I don't have to scrunch up my shoulders too much, and the ground is really mushy. The bad news is that my shoes are sinking way down into it, which means that some red mud tennis shoes are gonna be part of my future for quite some time. No time to piss and moan, though, 'cause I damn sure don't want to be modeling them for Mama in the next few minutes.

More time goes by and my knees are throbbing like a rabbit's dick. I want to stand up so badly and stretch them out, but doing that could quickly spell the end of this game. If my head tops the crest of this ditch, I might very well be enjoying a red clay sandwich for lunch. And dried up nail polish for dessert. So my knees are just gonna have to keep right on aching.

Five or six more minutes go by, but finally I slowly stand up and look up over the top of the ditch. I've hit the jackpot! I spot Brother easing himself down into a ditch that's just two over from where I am. The best thing is, he pretty well has his back to me, so he doesn't even know I've seen him. I have his ass just where I want him!

I duck down and count off a couple of minutes—literally count them off, one thousand one, one thousand two, etc. The reason I'm doing this is that I figure that as soon as Brother gets down into his ditch, he will ease his head up a tad in order to take a look around. And if I happen to make the mistake of crawling up over into the next ditch when he does that, well, this game will be somewhat over. No, dammit to hell, over. Some red clay and I would now be closely bonded together. So I figure now that he's crouching low and moving towards the other side of the ditch, it's the perfect time to make my move.

I take a short little hop upwards to get on top of the ground that runs from my ditch over to the next one. Once I get my body up there, I only have a couple of feet to crawl to get over to the next ditch, which will put me only one away from Brother's. I crawl really, really slow, 'cause there's no room for error. If I make just a tiny bit of noise, Brother will look up and my ass will be deader than Napoleon, Hitler, and Stalin's all put together. I've gotta keep quiet, keep crawlin', and pray like a mantis that this works out the way I want it to.

I do make it, and I don't even make much noise when I ease down into this new ditch! What's making me feel even better is that I'm hearing a little rustling over in the next ditch, just a few feet down from me. Now, like a wildcat, it's time to stalk my prey. I find a nice palm-sized rock, which in these rock-lined ditches is easier than finding a rubber machine in a bus station. I'm serious, there are rocks all over hell and haddock out here. My plan is to take it and throw it over towards a small pine tree that's right close to where I just heard this noise. If I have just a gnat's ass amount of luck here in my corner, Brother will either jump or flinch, and then his ass belongs to me.

I pick up my rock, blow on it a tad to knock the dust off, and draw my arm back to release the stony missile. For once in my life I make an almost perfect throw and rattle the hell out of some of the pine tree's lower limbs. I almost think I hear some movement, so it might make sense to lob yet another stony grenade over in that same direction. This time, though, I'm determined to do even better. It takes me maybe fifteen or twenty seconds, but I find this really, really big chunk of dried out red mud. It's almost the size of a basketball, and I figure that Brother's ass can right now become truly mine. All it'll take is lobbing this crumbling baby right over in his general direction again, but this time I'll lob it right into the ditch he's hiding out in. The way I figure it, even if I don't score a direct hit I might still score a kill just from the size of the explosion of this titanic-sized chunk of clay. It's really dry, and just the perfect consistency to bust up and splatter all over hell.

I ease forward a couple of steps, and using both arms, heave this huge chuck of dirt right over into Brother's ditch. It lands in just a second or two and makes one helluva *"CLUMP."* I can clearly hear the clay chunks busting up from the impact. Hell, there's no way Brother didn't take some red shrapnel from that. The only problem is I don't hear any sounds coming from his ditch. It's sorta strange. I would think he would've at least cussed a little, so I figure I need to take a quick look over towards his ditch to see if I can detect any movement. Don't get me wrong. I'm not gonna do anything stupid, but I need to see what the hell is going on here. I decide to get up on my tiptoes and start lookin' around when something pecks the back of my left shoulder really hard. I turn around quickly and see that a quarter-sized piece of rock is lying there on the ground—one that wasn't there just a moment or so ago. And when I do the natural thing and look upwards…

…a rocket of dried mud pops me hard right in the face and busts up all over my nose, eyes and mouth! It stuns the hell out of me and I fall over backwards, right into a soft, red muddy spot, close to where I was just standing. That's bad enough, being laid out on the ground in a bunch of soft red mud, but what happens next is even worse. Another chunk of red clay, this one a tad smaller, zaps through the air like a guinea wasp and hits me right in the britches. Hard. And not just right in the britches, but right close to where my pink love poker and cardsack happen to reside—basically, I've been nailed right here on the dick with another big, hard piece of red clay. Fortunately, my jeans are pretty thick and absorb some of the blow. Still, I get a slightly queasy feeling and grab my nuts just to make sure they're still intact. And that's how I'm laying here on the ground, my eyes, nose and mouth full of red mud, with both hands holding my reproductive organs, when Brother walks up. Well, I guess he walks up, cause I can't see much of anything due to my currently clay-impaired vision, but I can sure hear him laughing. Laughing hard, and directed straight at me…

"Man, what a hit!"

I respond the only way I can—with a good, ole groan. A heartfelt one, too.

Brother laughs like you do when the singer at a funeral is really bad, and asks, "Gee, did that one direct to the balls suck a little of the wind out of you? Or are you just glad to see me?"

In normal times, I would pop his ass good for a comment like that, but it's funny how having clay-caked eyeballs and a cardsack that feels like a bunch of bees have stung it alters your disposition. I just grunt back at him, then try to look up. But when I do, the dirt in my eyes stings really, really bad, so I just have to say to hell with dignity, close my eyes, and cup my nuts with both hands until the stinging wears off. Finally, the tears flooding out of my eyes wash the dirt out to the point that I can squint one open and see. When that happens, I ask Brother just how big that first clump of mud had been. He tells me it was about two thirds of the size of a basketball, which explains why my hair, face, chest, arms, torso, groin, legs and feet are all covered with a dusting of red clay. To tell ya'll the truth, when my other eye finally clears up and I can fully see, I start laughing. I mean, the only thing around here that has more red mud on it than me are these damn ditches that we're sitting in. Brother starts laughing, too, and now we're having a great time, reliving the whole game and who did what. One question that I've absolutely got to ask Brother was how he had managed to get behind me and surprise me like he did.

He answered, "Well, everything you kept throwing over at me kept landing just a few feet in front of me. I figured that if I just snuck back up a few feet the other way, got out and came up behind you, that you would never have a clue. Well, at least never have a clue until you were tasting a good bit of red clay. And it looks like I was right on the money, don't it?"

Smartass. But I do have to hand it to him, he was right

on target. And I'll give him some more credit, as he's being a good guy and helping me knock a lot of this red clay off of me and my clothes. All the good feelings I'm building back up for him get dashed, though, when he says, "Well, by the time we walk back up to the house it ought to be about lunchtime. And I'm sure gonna enjoy watching you 'fess up to Mom about being out here in this pasture throwing around chunks of red mud!"

I take back what I just said about him, he's actually an orange-haired, double smart-assed jerk. The bad thing is, though, that he's right. There's nothing left for me to do but work my way back up through all this brush, and go face the music. So that's what Brother and I proceed to do. We dust ourselves off as best we can and begin working our way back up towards our house.

We have to walk through some slick leaf-covered limbs and shit in order to get there, which is just peachy, but we ultimately make our way back into the yard relatively unscathed. I should've bet a lot of money on this, 'cause this is how it always works out. Mama walks out of the house and into the yard just as the two of us are walking up. She looks over at Brother, then at me, and when she sees me her face gets this look on it like someone has just told her that she could never have any more iced tea and would have to drink Geritol in its place. I haven't even gotten within twenty yards of her when the shit starts hitting the fan.

"Son, what in the devil do you have on you, half the red mud in Juliette? Do you think that I spend time in front of the washing machine cleaning your clothes for you just to run out into the woods and mess them up? I swear, I work and work and work and work, and do I ask for much of anything? No! Do I ask you boys to help me clean up around this house? No! Do I ask you to button up the top button of your shirts at dinner? No! But the one thing I do ask for is something that ya'll disregard over and over and over again, and that's to keep your tails clean. Edward, since you seem to have a real problem with that, your reward is going to be two potted meat sandwiches for lunch. Ernest and I will clean up the rest of that country ham we had for dinner last night."

Potted meat sandwiches. The bad thing about potted meat is that I have no idea what the hell is in it. It's this mushed-up, weird-colored shit that could be anything, and probably is. My buddy Vee Huckabuck once told me that it's pieces of meat that they can't use in regular meat products like cold cuts and sausage. That's bad enough, but then Ted Strickland chimed into our conversation and told me something even worse. He told me that potted meat was made of stuff like ground up horses and dogs' dicks, and the intestines of diseased sheep for added flavor. It was enough to make you barf up chunks and, needless to say, I haven't been begging for potted meat too much lately. But, whatever kind of ground up dicks are in it, the fact is that I'm going to be eating two sandwiches' worth. And the bad thing is that there's no way in hell that I can raise any fuss about it because Mama is mad at me right now. All I can hope for is that those horses and dogs had relatively clean dicks the day they happened to pass on to their respective Oscar Meyer and Jimmy Dean heavens.

We both go on in the house, wash up, and sit down to eat our lunches. Actually, things don't turn out as bad as I thought they would. I manage to choke one sandwich down, and I convince Mama that the second sandwich has some bread on it that is real close to being moldy. She lets me throw the second sandwich out the back door, and Mary the Puppy Dog catches the thing in mid-air before it even touches the ground. She gulps it down in two big bites, and doggie smiles real big while she does. In the past I've never been happy if someone ate something that belonged to me, but I have a heart full of forgiveness going for Mary right now. Dogs really are a guy's best friend.

Not a whole lot else happens the rest of the day. Mama gets caught up in her soap operas and I actually reread my favorite biography, one about Thomas Edison. Edison has to be one of the coolest guys of all time. Here's a guy that was pretty near deaf, and everyone thought he was stupid when he was growing up. His teachers got on to him for asking lots of questions in class, and some of them even made fun of him. He went on from that and became the greatest inventor of all time. I love his positive outlook, which embodied itself in his work on the light bulb. It seems that he had the hardest time coming up with a filament that would last. He tried all sorts of threads, horse hairs, sheep's wool, just about anything. None worked, but did that get him down? Hardly. In one interview, he was asked about being frustrated after trying all those materials but gaining no success, and he responded by pointing out that he now knew that those particular materials wouldn't work. He turned a negative situation into a real positive one, all due to his outlook. Basically, as Ed Jr. put it, he didn't whip his own ass. He believed in himself, and ultimately, he achieved. I'll bet that most of those people who laughed at him back then probably own their own copies of his biography now.

Anyway, I spend the whole afternoon reading, and gettin' sort of lazy feelin' until Ed Jr. comes home from work. He is actually a little late getting here, coming in around five instead of his usual four-thirty. How he comes in is what makes it all really weird. He has this almost pale look about him when he comes in, and he gathers all of us together and tells us that what he is about to tell us is true, and that he will stake everything he has on it. I've never been so surprised. In fact, he is so deathly serious that he tells us, "…if every word of what I'm about to say here isn't true, I'll give up watching the Super Bowl. For good. And I mean it." Mama, Brother, and I know when he says that, that something pretty serious has happened.

It turns out that indeed it has. As we gather around him, Ed Jr. starts telling us that he had just been out driving on the dirt road that runs up to our house when he saw this old colored guy walking alongside the road. He said that he almost couldn't believe who he was seeing, because it looked just like a man he had known years ago, called Uncle Dock. Ed Jr. said that Uncle Dock had lived in these parts all his life, and that he loved two things more than anything else—whiskey and women. Apparently Uncle Dock had been married two or three times, and normally kept one wife and maybe three or four girlfriends on the side at all times. Ed Jr. added that several pretty interesting situations happened along the way when Uncle Dock's wife would catch him out with one of his girlfriends. According to Ed Jr., one night Uncle Dock's wife was supposed to have caught him over at the Rocket Inn with some female companionship. Walked right up on the two of 'em in the bar and confronted 'em right in front of everybody. In the heat of the moment, Uncle Dock's girlfriend told his wife, "And why shouldn't he spend some money on me? I'm fresh, and the only fresh thing he has to look forward to in ya'll's house is the current loaf of bread you is usin'." Needless to say, Uncle Dock's wife hauled off and popped his girlfriend hard across the chops over that, and that started a ruckus that ended up takin' a couple of Sheriff's deputies to break up. And even when the deputies got the two women apart, the girlfriend yelled over to Uncle Dock's wife that "Satan has more of a grip on Jesus than you do on this man, 'cause he be mine." That caused Uncle Dock's wife to pick up a kerosene lantern that was sittin' out on the table and chunk it right at her. Fortunately, the girlfriend ducked, and she proceeded to laugh her ass off about it. Then she remarked that the less light there was in there the better it was for Uncle Dock's wife as no one could see her "dog tired, giraffe look-alike face" there in the bar. That caused the two of them to lock up yet one more time, and the deputies had to pry them apart again. Only the promise of some serious jail time finally calmed the two passion-filled combatants down.

Ed Jr. says that there are at least another twenty stories like this about Uncle Dock. He then says that he needs to tell us what had just happened, and the sooner the better. He adds that we might think he's crazy or loopy based on what he is about to say, but he says he would swear on a Bible and Vince Lombardi's good name that every word he is about to say is true. Mama, Brother and I can only nod in response, and then the three of us get real quiet and listen to what the old man just has to get out of his system.

"I'd just topped over the hill towards the house in the Falcon when I saw this old man walkin' alongside the road. At first, I didn't think too much about it, just figured it was one more old colored man walking alongside the road 'til I got up close to him. When I did, I almost thought my eyes were lying to me, but even after blinking a couple of times, I kept seein' the same thing—Uncle Dock himself was walking alongside the road!"

I interrupt him, asking, "Gee Dad, what's the big deal about that? Lots of people walk alongside the road. Why would this guy be different than a zillion other people who do that?"

Ed Jr.'s answer clears things up when he says, "'Cause son, Uncle Dock died a good nine or ten years ago."

I think I'm hearing him wrong, and say, "You can't mean that."

He looks at me like I'm daft, a Democrat, or both, and replies, "Son, who in the hell would make up a story about a ten-year-old dead darkie walkin' alongside the road?"

I have to give him that one. Hell, I'm even starting to believe what he is saying at this point, and I don't want to slow him up any, so I figure the best thing to do is shut up and listen. And that's what I do.

"Son, I'm telling you, it's the damndest thing that's ever happened to me. I just can't understand it, I tell you. I had just topped over the hill, and right as I was coming down it, I saw this old guy walking real slow up towards our house. To tell you the truth, I knew it was Uncle Dock right away 'cause no one else walks like he does. I mean, it's sort of like he's riding a horse but there's no horse there, you know, his legs are all bowed out, sort of like parentheses. When he steps forward with his right leg, he leans way over to the right. When he steps forward with his left, he leans way left. So when he walks, you know that it's got to be him. It's like he's drunk but has full control of himself, all at the same time. It's sort of like his signature thing, his personal ID if you will.

"Anyway, I pulled up real close to him, rolled down the window, and asked, 'Is that you, Uncle Dock?' He smiled and told me right away that it was. Then I said, 'Uncle Dock, they told me you had died a good while back, that you'd taken ill, couldn't whip it, and ended up dead. You know, none of us have seen you in a damned long time, so we all believed it.'

"Uncle Dock looked right at me, thought for a second, and said back, 'Well son, I've been here and there, looked at this and that, but as you can see, I be here talkin' with you right now as we speak. No two ways about it, for sure, I is here.'"

At this point, Ed Jr. says that the polite thing to do was to ask Uncle Dock if he needed a lift, especially given the way he walked. "It'd take him a damned week to walk to the shithouse and back, and I'm bein' generous about it." He offered him the ride, and Uncle Dock accepted, climbing into the back seat of our old blue Falcon. Then, my dad says that he drove him about three miles or so on down McCrackin Street, until Uncle Dock asked him to veer right and to go down a very seldom-used little dirt road called Two Lip Lane. Ed Jr. took Uncle Dock just a few hundred yards into it when he asked him to stop. My dad says that he thought that his request was a tad unusual as there's nothing out on this little dirt road, absolutely nothing, no houses, no cars, nothing. Still, Uncle Dock wanted him to stop at that point, so he was a good guy and stopped. Uncle Dock then got out of the car, smiled, and thanked Ed Jr. for the lift. My dad says that the curiosity about where Uncle Dock was headed got to him, so he just came out and asked, "Uncle Dock, would you mind tellin' me where in the hell you're goin'? There's not a whole lot out here, and I would be glad to run you back into Juliette if you need me to." Uncle Dock's reply to that was something that Ed Jr. says he'll likely remember for a long time.

"Mistah Ed, I'll tell you exactly where I'm headed. I'm jes headed here and there, and so forth. I jes go where I needs to be. Thank you kindly, Mistah Ed, for the lift. I'll be takin' my leave now." And with that, Uncle Dock headed on down the road.

Ed Jr. says that he figured he better run back into Juliette real quick and let some of Uncle Dock's kinfolks know where he was. So, he headed the Falcon back downtown and did exactly that. As he cruised the main drag, Wig happened to be ambling along the side of the road. Ed Jr. immediately pulled over and told him he had just picked up Uncle Dock, and that he had left him out on the old dirt road that forks off McCrackin Street. He noticed that Wig was staring at him real funny while he was explaining all this, and when he finished, Wig said, "Mistah Ed, I know you to bees a man of your word, and I wants to believe everything that you is telling me here. But Uncle Dock, well, he has been dead for nigh close to ten years now. I saw him in his coffin and everything, when he was laid to rest. I wants to believe you, but I jes cain't, but I certainly mean no offense, sir. Your parents is fine people, and I has known you all me life. I don't know who you have just kindly driven up the road here, but it cain't be Uncle Dock. Unk Dock is as cold as one of them drink box dopes." And with that, Wig walked away.

We all look right at Ed Jr., and it's safe to say that he looks a tad bewildered. Okay, well, more than just a tad. He swears up and down that he had the conversation, and that the man involved had to be Uncle Dock. Finally, after hashing all this around for a good half hour or better, we decide to chalk it up to just one of those things that you'll never be able to explain or understand. Of course, down the road we might definitely have to rag out the old man's ass on this situation, but now is sure as hell not the time. Hell, he has me believing that all this happened, which is something I don't want to say out loud around anyone I know. All I can say is that if this is the way winter's starting out, it's gonna be a helluva one, and you can bet every RC Cola you have on it.

Two

November sucks just about as badly as any month of the year. In fact, it may be the worst month of all, if you really think about it. The weather gets all cold and dreary, school goes on pretty much the whole damned time, and all you can say good about it is that you get to eat really well a couple of days towards the end. And I'm real lucky regarding that, because we eat Thanksgiving once at our house, once at Ed Sr. and Miss Lily's, and then once at Grandpa and Sweetie's. That's a lot of good food, and some of it is the same, some of it is different.

Miss Lily, for example, makes the best biscuits you'll ever eat in your life. They're all flaky and hot, and just sort of crumble and melt in your mouth all at the same time. Her green beans can't be beat, either. It's a funny thing, green beans absolutely suck to me. Most times they taste pretty much like well water, which means that they have no taste at all. Bottom line, they're a worthless food item, right on a par with beets, figs, and rutabagas. Miss Lily, though, has gotten green beans down to a science, and it's on account of how she seasons them—hell, I find myself eating them like a skinny prisoner just to get down to that pot likker. God, does she make some good pot likker. I crave it like a pimp craves a weekend convention hittin' town. It has a nice sort of warm, buttery taste to it, with just the right amount of pepper sprinkled in. Give me a couple of her biscuits and some of that pot likker, and I'll eat like a king or a starving dog, whichever one makes the point to you folks out there the best.

Sweetie, on the other hand, makes some of the best turkey and dressing that you'll ever eat. I think she cooks the turkey for at least two or three days beforehand, because the meat will just about fall off the bones when it's actually carved. On top of that is her dressing—it's so good that I'm tempted to say that it's better than sex, although everyone knows that's a lie, but it still sounds pretty good. Sweetie's dressing is cooked so that it's golden brown on top and she always puts the just the right amount of seasoning into it. She also doesn't load it up with a bunch of celery and some of that other shit that I don't quite know what it is, that unknown dressing type shit, the lumps and all, you know. To be honest, I can take two or three good slices of turkey, a couple of healthy spoons full of dressing, and be one pretty damn content Williams boy.

Let's not even start talkin' about desserts. Miss Lily can whip up pies that are to die for; apple pies with just enough brown sugar on them to make your tongue dance around in your mouth. Sweetie makes a chocolate cake with icing on it so thick that it's just like having fudge poured all over the cake. On top of that, she'll lay pecans right into all that great frosting, which makes eating the cake itself almost like sex for the mouth. I could throw in a few words here about Miss Lily's peach cobbler, then counter back with Sweetie's carrot cake, and keep going on and on and back and forth for a pretty damned good while. Let's just say that when we eat Thanksgiving with Sweetie one day and Miss Lily the next, that my stomach is the absolute happiest it's gonna be all year.

Thanksgiving is gonna be good for me this year. We're all gonna actually eat together out at Ed Sr. and Miss Lily's, which is sort of a rare event in the Williams family. It's funny—we all pretty much get along, we all have fun when we see each other, but we hardly ever have one of these "let's all eat out at Grandma's on Sunday" type deals. And, to tell ya'll the truth, I'm pretty damn glad about it. I have a friend over at Mary Persons that always bitches and moans about having to eat Sunday lunch over at his grandmother and grandfather's every single Sunday. He says that twenty or thirty people usually show up, and the bad thing about it is that there's only one bathroom for all of them to use. He says that you can count on at least one child having a bad case of the squirts, which makes the bathroom off limits to everyone else. If you're unfortunate enough to have a bad pain hit you while you're there, well, all you can do is ease out the back door and trot off towards the woods. That's not the most terrible thing in the world to have to do unless it's winter, and I don't care whether you have to crap or piss, dangling your love poker or your ass out in twenty-degree cold is not my idea of a good time. In addition to that, he tells me that his grandparents' house is heated with space heaters and that his grandmother is real cold-natured. In the wintertime, he says that she'll have every damn space heater in the house revved up full blast, which means that the indoor temperature hovers at around one hundred and ten degrees. My buddy says that your choices are to either go outside and freeze your balls off, or to stay inside and have your body think that you're spending the day over in the tropics somewhere. It's definitely not the way he wants to spend his Sundays, and that's being kind about it.

It's not the way I want to spend mine, either, but guess what? We all have a pretty good time together this year. All my uncles, Dog, Jew, Bob, and Calhoun show up, as well as my Auntie Lorena. And on top of that, all of their spouses and kids attend as well. The adults all sit at the big dining room table, and I feel pretty good because I'm allowed to sit in there with them. To be honest, I'm really not sure why, unless it's the fact that I'm "the third", and therefore rate a spot at the main table of honor.

Whatever the reason, I enjoy being in there more than flies love constipated cows. There are like eight tons of food, stuff like fried chicken sitting alongside the turkey and dressing, and more side dishes than I've ever seen in my whole entire life. We have potato salad, mashed potatoes, sweet potato soufflé, stuffed celery, green beans, some kind of congealed Jell-O salad with cheese and sour cream like shit mixed into it, biscuits, corn bread, and about ten gallons of iced tea to slide it all down with.

And as if that weren't enough to make a pink-assed hog say grace, Miss Lily has brewed up some of her blackberry wine, which is the single best stuff in the whole world to sip on. She doesn't have any out on the table, but I know some is close by in her secret wine hiding place. She has actually slipped me a tad in the past when I've gone out to the Byars Place to visit her, so I've actually had more than just a tad, but that's a secret between me and her. I just love Miss Lily to death. She has tons of common sense about her, and a whole lot of spark to boot. Hell, let's face it, the old girl has enough piss and vinegar inside her to float the Titanic, and I couldn't love her more than I do. I think I'd even like Miss Lily if she weren't related to me in any way at all.

Hmm, I'm getting a tad ahead of myself here. I think I ought to tell ya'll how I know that Miss Lily has made up some blackberry wine, especially since none was out in plain view and all. What tips me off is that during the course of dinner Uncle Dog keeps going back and forth into the kitchen, and each time he returns, he's smiling even bigger than the time he'd gone before. I finally pick up on the fact that something is going on when he winks real big right at one of our married-into-the-family aunts that he doesn't like much at all. When I see that, I know that something shifty is going on, and when I look over at Miss Lily, she gives me a smile that pretty much confirms what my gut is tellin' me. I figure that it's not my concern anyway, and I know that I'd better focus and fend for myself or all the food is going to be gone faster than Butts County women drop their britches.

Ya'll have to understand that when the Williamses eat it's almost like a semi-polite free-for-all. Plates of food are going all around the table in different directions, and you almost laugh out loud at all the noises that come from the spoons clanking against bowls, dishes clattering down on the table, and from all the "pleases" and "thank yous" and "damn right I want some mores" that are constantly ringing out all around the table. I've learned that you have to get right in there with them and deal, 'cause if you don't, you'll end up hungry and not one soul there will feel the least bit sorry for you. The Williamses are as good an example of survival of the fittest as you'll ever find, and I'm pretty damn glad of it. Believe me, I realize that I could've been born into some pansy family just as easily as I was into this one, but who wants to be raised by Ward and June Cleaver? Not me, believe me, not me.

Once all the food has been circulated around, the real eating begins. It's funny watching how people eat, if you sit and give it some thought. Some of them will eat a little bit of everything on their plates, and then you have others that will eat all of one item before they'll move on to something else. I guess each to his or her own, but I sort of wonder about those "eat one thing completely before you eat anything else types." Almost seems like something a Communist would do, or at the very least a Socialist. I think Ed Jr. is pretty much on the money when he tells me that there are some things in life that we'll just never understand, these Commie one-item eaters being amongst them.

The forks and knives and spoons are clanking something fierce, and I notice that the fried chicken is getting hit just as hard as the turkey is. Uncle Calhoun especially prefers the chicken. To prove it, he has both a drumstick and a breast on his plate, but no turkey. Uncle Bob calls him out on that, and Uncle Calhoun replies that turkey has no taste to it at all and that he would just as soon deep sniff a bat's ass as eat some. Miss Lily sort of gets on to him for talkin' about a bat's ass right there at the table, but it just inspires Dog to speculate on the odds of even getting close enough to a bat to see its ass, much less sniff it. This brings forward some laughs and chuckles, but it also makes Ed Jr. frown a little. He remarks that the thought of a tiny black bat's ass is not making his dinner very appealing, and that they should talk about something that everyone agrees on, like how ugly both of President Johnson's daughters are. Everyone pretty much nods in agreement over this, and this leads to Ed Sr. giving us some of his thoughts on haints in general.

He is just starting to get into some dialogue about some old gal who Dog had once dated who had large boobs, "but a face that would scare an ice cream truck away," when something a little out of the ordinary happens. Wig, an old colored guy that spends most of his days sitting on the porch outside of Ed Sr.'s store, pulls up into the driveway in the most raggedy Chevrolet that you've ever seen in your life. It's some kind of old model Chevy sedan, and you can hardly tell what color the paint job is due to all the dirt, mud, and dust caked up on it. Wig obviously doesn't believe in washing it. Hell, I think Wig might be afraid that the car would fall apart if the mud was ever removed, so he just leaves it on there. Whatever the reason, the bottom line is that he was driving up to Ed Sr.'s house in a raggedy old car right in the middle of our Thanksgiving dinner. Needless to say, Ed Sr. is not happy over this at all, and he wasn't shy about saying so.

"Goddammit! Here we are celebrating a special time, and Wig is bringin' his old darkie ass right up here to our house. If luck was money, I couldn't buy a damned gumball! I'll guarantee ya'll one damn thing, he wants something, you can bet your asses on it. May be money, some tools, food, or maybe it's something else. I would bet my lily-white patootie on it, damn the luck!"

After saying these tender words, he gets up out of his chair and makes his way out into the front yard. Ed Jr., Dog, Calhoun, and I all get up and follow him. I guess we are all nosy and want to hear what Wig is gonna say. It doesn't take us very long to find out, as Wig pulls up within a few feet of where we all are standing. He then stops his car, turns off the engine, and gets out. After dusting himself off some with both his hands, he walks up to Ed Sr., who nods at him, and then Wig begins the conversation with the following:

"Mistah Ed, I am shore glad to see you. Expecially on sech a fine day as this. We all is very thankful today, and I am shore thankful for knowing such a fine family as you Williamses. A man can never have too many friends Mistah

Ed, and one reason why I is here is to tell you how much I appreciate you, Miss Lillian, these fine boys, and anyone else that is close to you. I jes want you to know that."

Ed Sr., surprisingly, takes all this pretty well. He nods at Wig, and Wig continues, "I do has another reason to be here as well. I was jes wonderin' if you might has a pair of jumper cables that I can borry. I ain't borrying them for me, Mistah Ed. I is borryin' them for my sistah, Louisa Mae. Louisa, as you know, she has them four chirrens, and one of dem is sick from something more bad than a cold. Little Chantice, you might remember her, is de bad sick one. She has been sneezin' and blowin' snot for damn near over a week now. From what I can see, what she has is more than a cold. Mistah Ed, I really thinks I needs to get her to Forsyth to see the doctor, but, I has been stuck with this one problem. And that problem is that Louisa has her old Lincoln, and she be coughin' and sputterin' like a mule fed on crabapples. And my fear is, Mistah Ed, is that we ain't gonna be able to get little Chantice to the doctor for some hep. Mistah Ed, all I need is the loan of some jumper cables. If you will loan them to me, I will bring them back soon. I hope that since today is Thanksgiving Day that you will bring some glad tidings for me and little Chantice."

You can tell that Ed Sr. doesn't know quite what to do or say but, after staring hard at Wig for a few seconds, he replies, "Wig, I got one set of jumper cables here at the house. You can borrow them all you want to, but I want 'em back, and soon. If I have to get up one cold morning and not be able to get one of my cars cranked, I'm gonna tie a four-square knot in your pit-black ass!"

Wig nods and says, "Mistah Ed, dem cables will be back by Sunday at de latest. You can bet everythin' and den some stump liquor on it."

Isn't much to be said after that. Ed Sr. sends me out to his office to fetch his jumper cables. I run down there, pull open the door and see them dangling over a nail that he'd hammered up into the wall. I take them down and shag ass back pretty quickly, as I figure every minute that goes by that

Ed Sr. has to deal with Wig and not eat his dinner is pretty much a wasted minute. Not to mention that I think he might get tired of waiting, and just go ahead and tell Wig to kiss his ass and go home. For some reason, that doesn't seem to be a good Thanksgiving Day-type thing for anyone to do, so I double time those cables over to Ed Sr.

He takes them from me, grimaces, and then turns around and faces Wig. Holding the cables out to him, he says, "Wig, these are the only damn jumper cables I have here at the house. I expect them back exactly when you said you'd have 'em back—this Sunday!"

Wig nods respectfully and replies, "Mistah Ed, dey will be back here Sunday, and you can take it to the bank. May the good Lord smite me clean into Alabama iffin' I don't live up to my word."

Ed Sr. nods, then says, "Dammit Wig, I've got to get back to the table now. Biggest meal of the year and I'm out here pissin' around with you over some damned jumper cables." Funny thing is, Wig seems to totally understand his point, and even seems to agree with him. Smiling at us all, he gets back into his old piece of shit car and backs it all the way out of our driveway. He then straightens it out once he gets back out into the main road, and is gone in a cloud of red Georgia dust quicker than a whore winks at a sailor.

Ed Sr. says nothing else, goes straight back into the house and sits back down at the table. The rest of us do the same. Miss Lily asks Ed Sr. what Wig wanted, and he replies that, "His sorry smoky ass wanted my jumper cables. Now, he had a good story, I'll give him that, a bunch of bullshit about his sister's kid needin' to go to the doctor. I went along with it just because it's Thanksgiving, and I don't think it's right to jump hard on a man's ass on Thanksgiving, no matter how much he may deserve it. I imagine, if the truth be known, that Wig's rag of a car won't start without being jumped off and that he thinks he'll get my jumper cables and I'll just forget about it. Well I won't, and I'm not above snatching a knot in his coal-black ass if those jumper cables don't show back up here when they're supposed to!"

Everyone at the table nods in agreement with that, and Miss Lily even says that there is a little bit of a Thanksgiving message in what Ed Sr. had just said, if you just think about it. Personally, I'm still sitting here thinking hard about what that might be, but I'm guessing it might be one of those things that only women and preachers understand. Anyway, we all get back to eatin' dinner, and the knives and forks are flyin' all around again, and everything seems to be gettin' back to normal.

After everyone has gotten another ten or fifteen minutes worth of eatin' done, Miss Lily hits her fork up against her glass to get our attention and tells us all that we should be thankful to be together on this day, and to be enjoying dinner like we all are. We all sort of look at each other and nod our heads in agreement. Then, Miss Lily reminds us that tomorrow is the start of the Christmas season, and how happy Christmas has made her over the years. I can understand what she means by that. Christmas is one of the coolest times in the world for most people, but it seems to have an even more special meaning here in Juliette. Just about every home around here gets all decorated up, and even the poorest families somehow manage to wind up with a few gifts for those special to them under their trees. Our two churches here, the Baptist and Methodist, both have special services, and they normally hand out gifts to all the young people that attend them. I loved that when I was little because it was almost like getting a part of your Christmas early, but as I got older, things changed. These last two or three years, all I've gotten is some cheap ass cologne, and this past year I got this huge chunk of soap on a rope. I've really never seen or heard of such a thing before, and when I showed it to Ed Jr., he remarked that "sweet guys use this, if you get my drift." That alone made me want to throw it away pronto, but Mama said that it was good soap and that I was not to be wasteful. So, given that, I used it all up in about a week, and I did so on purpose. I mean, I was soaping myself up two and three times each bath, and I would even leave the soap in the water the whole time I was in the tub to melt it down as much as possible. I washed really hard behind my knees a couple of times, which is one place that I never typically wash. Bottom line, I would've done whatever it would've taken to get rid of that soap, 'cause between Mama forcing me to use it and Ed Jr. and Ernest ragging out my ass about it, it just wasn't worth keeping it in play for very long, and that's for sure.

Anyway, Christmas is a great time around these parts, and Miss Lily goes on to say that we are fortunate to have most of our family here around the table on Thanksgiving Day. She then says that a good family way to start out the Christmas season would be for one of us to tell everyone a story about something special that they'd done at a Christmas in their past. Several hands go up around the table, but Ed Jr. says that he has a story to tell about Christmas that would set the tone for all of us this upcoming holiday season. Everyone nods at him and smiles, and we all kick back to listen to him share some tender Christmas memories with us. His story is as follows:

"Christmas can be special wherever you are, whether you're at home or at some other place, even if that place is somewhere far, far away from Juliette. Like a foreign country. And that's what I'm gonna tell ya'll about, a Christmas that I spent over in a foreign land…"

I already figure from that alone that this would have something to do with Korea. You see, Ed Jr. served in the Korean War for about fifteen months in 1951-52, and it's the only time he's ever departed from the United States. Hell, from what I can tell, it's one of the few times he's ever even departed from Georgia. I've asked him more than once why he doesn't like to get out more and see the world, and he always replies, "Why would I want to go off somewhere, eat some strange ass food, not know where anything is, and then have to pay for the privilege? The worst part of it is that I don't like to use a strange toilet. No telling whose ass has been on them, or what has been on them, and I aim to be healthy and live a long, eventful life. If someone wants to travel all over the place, that's fine, then they should just declare themselves a Gypsy and flit around wherever they want to. But leave my healthy ass out of it—I'm as Georgian as Senator Dick Russell, and you don't think that you'll ever see him moving to another state, now do you?"

I have to give him the benefit of the doubt regarding his logic on that one. And now I gotta get back to Ed Jr.'s Christmas story, cause he's talkin' fast and I'll miss it if I don't pay attention.

"I was over in Korea in '51 and part of '52, fighting it out with those godless gook bastards over there, and believe me, it was no damned walk through the daisies. I was over there for one full winter, and it was the coldest weather that I've ever experienced. Most nights it would drop down into the teens, or even get below zero. It was so cold that we were out doing reconnaissance one night and one of my buddies got out of the back of our jeep to take a piss. Honest to God, with all of you here as my witnesses, the piss froze right after it left his dick and stopped before it even hit the ground. Damndest thing I've ever seen and then some—an ice piss sculpture!"

Miss Lily clears her throat pretty loudly, which causes Ed Jr. to look at her. When he does, she shoots him a very serious look. I take that to mean that she feels her eldest son is telling something that isn't quite genteel enough for the ladies who are present, and that he needs to tone it down just a tad. He actually mumbles an apology to all the ladies and then goes on with his story. And, I'll give him credit; he stays subdued for a good couple of minutes or so, as ya'll can see here.

"What was about as bad as the cold was those Koreans themselves. They weren't bad people as a whole, they have a decent number of good qualities, but they are as poor as Job's turkey. They have a hard time feeding themselves, they seldom can find work, and they breed like rabbits, which makes their whole situation just that much worse. On account of that, they were always coming up to us wanting some food. We did our best to try and help them out, but sometimes all we had was a few cans of C-rations to get by with, and you couldn't give them the only damn food that you had. One time I had one of them Korean men get real upset with me when I wouldn't give him some of my food, so he got right up in my face and said a whole bunch of angry soundin' Korean shit to me. I didn't know what in the hell it meant, but I knew it wasn't good and I don't let a regular American get in my face and cuss me, much less a hungry gook. At that point my honor was at stake, so I popped him with a hard right hand to his chin, which taught him a good bit of respect. We got along right well after that.

"One day we were ordered by our superiors to take a group of trucks and armored vehicles up to the top of a large mountain. I forget the name of it, something like Mount Fit-Si-Reff-Wo-Fang or whatever, which is just as well because what normal person could pronounce it anyway? But we were supposed to get up on top of it and check out the surrounding area for North Korean hide-outs and shit. We all got together that morning and started loading up the trucks and getting them combat ready, 'cause we didn't know for sure just how long we would be up there and you've gotta have plenty of supplies just in case. We loaded them up with stuff like binoculars, blankets, food supplies, toilet paper, and especially with our sleeping bags. With all the snipers hiding out in those hills, there was always a chance that you might find yourself having to spend the night in the back of a convoy truck. And let me tell you, a night in Korea can get so damn cold that even inside a truck and zipped up inside a sleeping bag you can get so chilled that your ass puckers up like a yellow caution light!"

At this point, Miss Lily says, "Son, your language!"

Ed Jr. looks sort of sheepish, apologizes to his mother, and continues, "Well, we finally loaded up all those trucks about as full as we could get them, and we were about ready to take off when a couple of stray Koreans walked out of the jungle. They smiled and patted their stomachs, and we knew that they wanted food. Our sergeant went inside the mess tent and came back out with some old dried out beef jerky. I don't know where they got this damned jerky from, but it was so tough that you could've used it to rope a calf. Anyway, he tossed some long ass strands of it over to those Koreans, and they nodded so much that I was afraid that one of them was gonna get dirt on his chin.

"They went away right after that, and our sergeant told me and Lucky Wilson to get up into the first truck. We liked that because the very first truck in our convoy was the one that towed that big fifty."

I look around the table, and I can tell that several of us sitting there have not a clue as to what Ed Jr. means about a "big fifty," so I clear my throat and ask him if he would tell us.

He immediately responds, "Son, a big fifty is a fifty-caliber machine gun. It was the gun we took with us when something heavy was goin' down, when we damn well meant business. When your ass is going to the top of a big mountain with a bunch of militant North Korean rice burners lurking around out in the woods, a big fifty is a mighty good friend to have along for the ride!"

I can't dispute that logic. Miss Lily jumps in again and urges Ed Jr. to get on to the Christmas part of his story, which I am starting to wonder a little about myself. He dutifully nods, smiles at his mom, and continues:

"Lucky and I got up in that big truck, warmed up the engine, and waited for the signal to start rollin'. Lucky liked to drive, so he was at the wheel, and my job was to keep a sharp eye peeled for anything that looked strange. Believe me, you didn't have to let your attention lapse but for just a second or two, and then a North Korean would send your ass either to the promised land or to shake hands with Satan, whichever situation fitted you the best.

"The signal was then given, and all of the trucks and jeeps that were going lined up. Then another signal was given, and we started goin' up the mountain. At first, things weren't too bad, the road was level and plenty wide enough for us. After that, though, it got a little more tricky. The higher up we wound around the side of the mountain, the more gullies and shit that had washed their way through the road. Then, the road got skinnier and skinnier as it went even higher, and it got pretty damned high, so much so that I was lookin' over the side and saw nothing but a long ass drop that went so far that you could barely see the bottom. To be honest, I was gettin' about as skittish as a bean eater does at church, and with good reason. The higher up we kept goin', the more I noticed that our truck had no room for error. The road had no more room on either side of it, so if Lucky twitched at the steering wheel there was a damned good chance that me and him both were gonna go on to that great rice paddy in the sky with a truck bumper lodged up our asses. And that's not good no matter how you happen to look at it."

At this point, Miss Lily almost does another big throat clearing, but I think she looks around and sees how closely we're all listening to Ed Jr.s' Christmas overseas experience, so she keeps quiet. And Ed Jr. keeps right on talkin'.

"Didn't bother Lucky a damn bit, though. Hell, he even goosed the gas a little, just to make me squinch up to the point that I was damn near sucking up the truck seat with something other than my lips. Hell, I just about had to threaten to take a yard out of his ass to make him quit doing that, but he finally did and I was grateful. Grateful or not, though, I would've had to Joe Lewis his ass had he done that anymore."

Uncle Dog, who at this point had sucked down several additional swigs of blackberry wine, interrupts this tender story and asks, "Wolf, when do we get to the Christmas spirit part? I either want to have the sweet spirit of Jesus wash over me, get drunk, or both. Which one is it gonna be?"

Ed Jr. replies that he is real close to bringing Jesus into the picture, and continues, "We'd gotten about two-thirds of the way up the side of that mountain, and then we had to slow down. I couldn't hardly stand to look over the side, but for some godforsaken reason I finally did. And I have to admit that it was beautiful—the side of the mountain was all covered with snow, and the valley underneath was dotted out with trees and little inlets like ponds. It looked like something off of one of those made in Japan Christmas cards that has the real looking nature scenes and then an elf painted right on top of them. What I saw being without the elf, of course. You could see a few Koreans at the bottom of the mountain. They were milling around and foraging for food. Wintertime is pretty damned hard on them. The ground is frozen so solid that you can't grow anything, so all they have to eat is meat. And they will eat any damned meat that you put out there in front of them—dogs, cats, rabbits, skunks, anything that has four legs and runs. I felt pretty damned sorry for them, to tell you the truth, it must be pure hell to be Korean, cold, hungry, and wet."

Calhoun breaks in at this point and comments that it would be even worse to be a Yankee, cold, hungry, and wet, and have to live in New Jersey. We sort of laugh at this, as it is half-ass funny, until Ed Jr. gives us all a stern look. He then continues:

"I kept on looking around, and finally I looked up. I guess that's when it hit me as to how huge this mountain really was. We'd been driving a good while and still had a third of the way up it to go, which is still a damned long ways up. The air was so cold that it was bathing and freezing my eyeballs all at the same time. Still, it was the best scenery you could ever imagine—the mountain peak itself covered over with snow, rocks and outcroppings of the mountain jutting out of the white. It's hard to describe something that looks so good. It just pleases you somewhere inside, you know? I was sort of surveying the whole situation when I sensed something moving. At first I couldn't make out what it was, and then everything got real still again. I was puzzled as hell, and figured I might better have my rifle out and ready, just in case. I pulled it out and cocked it, and got really, really still. The air stayed real quiet for a while, and then suddenly I saw some movement again! And then, I finally got a handle on what I was sensing. Up there on a ledge, maybe a hundred yards up and to my left, was a mountain goat. A big old mountain goat, with a rack on him bigger than President Johnson's ears, which means he could've pushed a bulldozer around with it. And it hit me when I saw him that I now had the means to make it a sweeter Christmas for those damn Koreans."

I can't help but blurt out, "A sweet Christmas for those

Koreans…how?"

Ed Jr. is just as fast on the draw in response, "I'll tell you exactly how. I told ole Lucky to steady the truck and to keep a sharp eye out for anything unusual that might be lurking around out there. Then I got out, climbed up on the back of that truck, and swung out that big fifty!"

Auntie Lorena jumps in and says, "You don't mean…"

Ed Jr. replies, "Well, yeah, I do mean. What I exactly mean is that I set that big fifty upwards and drew a direct bead on that damn mountain goat. It took me a second or two, but as soon as I got him focused right into the middle of those crosshairs, I squeezed the trigger!"

Needless to say, a few eyebrows are raised. The old man continues:

"It all happened faster than a gnat fart, and I guess only about twelve to fourteen bullets actually came out of that big fifty, but it was all I needed. That old goat stiffened up, almost like one of those slow motion football replays that you see on TV, and tumbled right over the side. He had to have dropped a good couple hundred yards or more in the air before he even touched the side of the mountain. Thing was, as soon as his carcass touched the ground, those Koreans were all over him like strippers on an eighty-year-old rich man. They had him butchered and sectioned up before his ass even stopped rolling." And with that, Ed Jr. stops talking, folds his arms, and then looks around the table at all of us.

We all look around at each other, wondering if he has any more story to tell. When it is obvious he doesn't, we all just sort of stare at each other and don't say anything at first.

Finally, I figure if no one else is gonna say it, I would. "Uh, old man, I may be missing something here, but I don't know that I see the Christmas message in your story."

Ed Jr. turns and looks at me like I'd just declared that Eleanor Roosevelt had recently been selected Miss Bikini USA. Staring me directly in the eye, he says, "Son, damn, do I have to draw you a map? Those skinny-ass Koreans were damn near starving out there in the snow, and who knows what would've happened to them had I not stepped in? Due to the soft spot that I have in my heart, I provided them with some food, literally some bounty from above, some manna from heaven, or whatever else you wanna call it. The bottom line is that Ed Williams, Jr. provided those piss poor starving Koreans with something to eat, and I did it out of the goodness of my heart! Right before Christmas, too!"

I guess it's safe to say that the general mood around the table is bewilderment, mixed in with a few quick laughs. We don't get to think or talk much more about it anyway, as Uncle Dog has been chowing down while this story is being told, and the net result is that he burps out loud, almost buzzsaw out loud, right there at the table, which diverts everyone's attention over to him. His burp also serves as sort of a closing dinner bell—everyone starts getting up from the table, thanking Miss Lily for such a great spread, and then we all begin making our ways out into the back yard and to our cars. I stop on the way out and give Miss Lily a hug, then I thank her for a great Thanksgiving.

She smiles and says, "Son, I'm glad you liked it. I hated some of the language in there, and I know you know that these boys can be a tad rough, but, underneath it all, they're good boys. They're Williamses, and despite whatever else may be said, they're men and that's something we can all be pretty thankful for most days."

I think I pretty much understand what she means by that, and then Ed Jr. hustles us all out to our car and on to the house. A hot tub bath, some late news on WMAZ, and my ass is in bed. And very glad to be. Let me tell ya'll, I saw Z's like a dead man, the only thing deader than me on this particular night is that poor old Korean mountain goat…

Three

I'm never gonna figure out women. That's trite as hell, and every man's biggest complaint, but it's as true as breaking wind after eating some raisin bran. Even more than that, I'm never gonna figure out why I react to women the way I do. I can't understand myself at all in this regard, and the more I think about it, the more confused I get. Someone must've knocked me upside the head when I was an infant or something, as it's about the only explanation I can give as to why I'm so muddle-headed when it comes to the fairer sex. I don't even want to go any more into it, to tell ya'll the truth, but I guess I ought to, as it's not fair for me to say all this shit and then not explain it more fully. I don't like to tease people unless there are big rewards in it for me later on, and ya'll can figure out that one on your own.

Let me start off with the women closest to me and then work outwards from that. My steady girlfriend is Jenny. I think, well, shit, I know that I love her. Love the hell out of her. I think about her most all the time, and then some, to the point that she's sort of like a billboard in my brain. She's pretty, but the best thing about her is that she's intelligent. That turns me on a bunch. Jenny can talk about anything you wanna talk about, politics, sports, religion, anything, and make a damn good case for her point of view. On top of that, she's pretty damn sensual. Nice lips, a sculpted body (from what I've seen of it) and pretty eyes. The best eyes. She can look at me with those big soft eyes and I'd damn near give her all my Elvis albums if she asked me to. Basically, Jenny fits me like a glove, and I'd marry her today if I could somehow figure out how to pay the rent for the two of us. And if I could somehow figure out how to do that and marry her, it would stand to reason that I would be getting in her britches most every night. God, I want to do that with her so bad, but Jenny has to be the nicest girl I've ever seen, which means that I have about as much chance of screwing her as I do of lubing the tube with one of Hugh Hefner's girlfriends. And that chance is a big, fat zero with a capital "Z" slapped right on the front of it.

So here's where it gets really confusing. I love Jenny, and I damn sure want her, but I get tired of wanting her and not being able to have her. So, sometimes that feeling spills over to another girl, let's say one like Candy. Candy is pretty, long blonde hair, nice bazookas, and she wears great clothes. They're not too dressy, not too sloppy, they're just right. She looks sort of like a nice fresh package of M&Ms. Ya'll know, like the shiny new bags of them that you see in grocery stores that you just die to tear open when you happen to walk by them. Candy is cute like one of those bags, and you just can't wait to get her alone so that you can get those clothes right off her. And the best thing is, she lets you get them off her most of the time, and pretty quickly to boot. Fooling around with Candy can get me about as close to heaven as one Juliette boy can get, but when it's all over heaven pretty quickly turns back to Hell. I hate to tell on myself like this, but when Candy and I get finished tulip honin' all I really want to do is get her on home and then go eat a hamburger or something.

See what I mean? I love one girl but can't have her, and I don't love the other but can tap her drawers almost anytime I choose. The bad thing is, it gets even more confusing. The other night I slipped out with Traci, a nice girl who's a grade behind me. Traci is pretty average looking but has tits that could nourish all of Cleveland. She also happens to wear some of the wildest colored tennis shoes that I've ever seen. She'll be wearing normal everyday clothes one day, like blue and gray stuff, and then have on some bright pink tennis shoes to go along with it. You just can't help but love it. The best thing about Traci is that she'll go out with me just about anytime I ask her. We might spend one evening just talking and horsing around, then on another night, she'll drop her drawers for me, no questions asked.

I guess these damn Williams' hormones are gonna end up sending me straight to hell, but what's a guy to do? I just happen to come from a family where the males love to lubricate their love engines, and we don't really even try to hide the fact that we do. And that works for us sometimes, if ya'll can believe that. Some girls almost seem to like it if you're forward with them and tell them that you want in their drawers. Traci is like that. We might go out three or four times and do regular date stuff, then I can walk up to her in the hallway and whisper, "Traci, if I don't get in your pants pretty soon I may start humping my living room rug." She'll giggle and nod at that, and pretty soon we find ourselves making out like two rabbits in a small hutch. I guess I just don't know quite how to put all of this right in my mind—I really like and respect Traci, I greatly love porkin' her, but I don't really love her. I do love Jenny, but I don't ever get to lube the tube with her. And I don't in the least love Candy, but I damn sure love getting her naked.

So where does love fit into all this, and just what does love really mean, anyway? Maybe I love them all in certain ways and should just accept that about myself. But lordy, it's sure gonna get me in some big trouble if I ever decide to get married some day, unless I can figure out how to be simultaneously married to four or five women all at the same time. There's some kind of screwed up religion that I read about a while back where they actually let you do that, so maybe I should do some more research and see about becoming a man of the cloth for them some day.

I guess I ought to mention before we go on much further that it's now early December, and it's also time to transition from love and sex into the fact that basketball has started up again at Mary Persons High School. What this means for me is that I now have to start attending the basketball pep rallies, which is a true bunch of shit—no one here gives a damn about basketball, it's a limp dick sport. Football is king here, and even the football pep rallies are kinda lame. So why would anyone give a shit about these lame ass basketball holleramas? Basketball pep rallies are even more boring than opera-loving preachers, and that's about as boring as things can get, unless you consider listening to Perry Como records, and I don't even have the time to explain just how damned sucky they are.

They herd all of us up around two o'clock this afternoon to go over to the gym and cheer on the basketball team. They're playing the Jackson Red Devils tonight, and they're the ultimate poster children for why incest is wrong. Most of the school shows up for it, but that's a gyp, because if you intentionally duck the pep rally they assign you a bunch of busy work that Cheetah the Chimp could be trained to do. Stuff like writing the same sentence down six thousand times in a row on the board, a technique which had to be thought up by Russian torturers. Anyone but the biggest pansies God ever created knows that it makes more sense to attend the pep rallies than to do that, so everyone in school goes. In fact, today's pep rally is so jammed out in the gym that you'd think something worthwhile is going on. Believe me, everyday piss ants have more going on than there is in that gym.

I'll try to describe it to ya'll as best I can without heavin'. The band queers come out to start things off, in formation no less, and they start trying to play some current popular songs. Needless to say, they just butcher the hell out of them. Let's face it, "These Eyes" is just not meant to be played with tubas and trombones, but try passing that message along to our band director—I think he figures that if they work hard enough that it might even start sounding good in spite of itself. But his logic just doesn't track. Tubas, at best, sound like educated farts, and a backdrop of high IQ farts doesn't really help out a song like "These Eyes." I can only imagine going to a Guess Who concert and breaking a big, loud fart while

Burton Cummings is singing "These Eyes." He'd be about as happy about that as I am to be sitting here in this gym.

After "These Eyes," the band actually launches into some Christmas music. The first couple of songs are really bad, but then they play "What Child is This?" and my whole mood changes.

I don't know why that song gets to me, but it just sort of catches me inside. I guess the Baby Jesus story and the whole deal around His birth is so improbable, I mean, who would guess that a baby lying around in a manger would go on to be the single most important person ever? I've always liked that aspect of Christmas, that Christ was born in very simple circumstances, spent his life with ordinary people, and did some things so stunning that people still talk about them today. Maybe that's why this song gets to me so much, the simplicity of Jesus' life, the way He lived it, and how bravely and nobly He faced His end. No matter how cool or whatever I may think I am, I always keep enough sense in me to know that I should honor Jesus.

This damn pep rally is going from bad to worse. After mauling every song except "What Child Is This?" the band starts playing Christmas carols quietly while the basketball cheerleaders read little stories or poems about Christmas over the PA system. It isn't too bad for the first few minutes, but with eight cheerleaders each reading for about four or five minutes it becomes both pond water slow and Pat Paulsen boring. It gets so bad that I start thinking about porno movies, farting, scratching, almost anything I can come up with to regain my sense of balance. I just can't imagine who thinks up the shit for these pep rallies, and I guess it's very telling that no one ever steps forward to take credit for any of it.

A weird thing happens while I'm sitting through all this shit that makes the whole damn thing worthwhile. I happen to be sitting up in the top of the gym with two of my good friends, Steven Davis and Gordon Watson. Gordon and I play football together, and Steven and I have been friends since our elementary school days. Anyway, we're just sitting around wondering when this school sanctioned toothache might end, and the wildest thing happens. I feel someone tug on my jacket sleeve, so I turn around and look. The person doing the pulling is Laurie Spencer, a cute blonde who happens to be a junior, if I remember last year's yearbook pics correctly. Laurie looks pretty hot in a pair of jeans and one of those Grateful Dead looking, flowery tie-dyed tops. I look at her, smile, and say hello. She responds as follows, "Hi. I really like how you look, would you like to kiss me?"

I honestly think she's bullshitting around, so I reply, "Run that by me again."

So she does, saying, "So, would you like to kiss me? You're cute."

I figure the only thing to do is say "sure," so I do. You have to figure that she's just bluffing or horsing around to get some attention. Those type thoughts are working their way around in my brain until I notice her leaning over, her face coming towards mine, and then I feel these very nice, soft little lips touch themselves against mine. This feels great in and of itself, and then the tip of her tongue dances around my lips, and I pull her close, realizing that she wants something more than a friendly, grandmotherly-type peck. I'm damn sure committed to seeing that she gets what she wants, so our kiss gets a tad more intense, and I'm almost at the point of copping a feel when a little reality slips into my brain. You see, I'm one of those types that like to sneak a glance or two at the girl while I'm kissing her, and that's what I do in this particular situation. The only thing is, when I do glance at her, I notice both Steven and Gordon and about thirty or forty other people staring straight at me. I don't mind telling ya'll that it cools down my jets a little, but it doesn't make a damn bit of difference to Laurie. She's kissing me like it was her last one before checking into a convent, but I can't enjoy it as much with all those sets of eyes glued on me.

Finally, Laurie notices that I'm not returning the kiss with my usual zeal, so she breaks it and sits back down in her seat. Leaning towards me again, she asks, "Baby, why did you stop? We were just getting started."

I stammer back, "Laurie, all these people are glaring at us. I love kissin' as much as anybody, but it could be a whole lot better in a little more private situation."

Laurie looks a tad funny, and then she casts a disdainful glance at all the people sitting around us. Then she looks back at me and says, really, really loud, "Ed, the only thing wrong with these shits is that they wish they were us. Don't let yourself be like them and end up all stove up, you just give me what I need and I promise you that what we'll do together later on will be even better."

Hell, a guard at Buckingham Palace would break under that kind of pressure, so I break ranks like a French regiment. We start kissing again, and some of my friends on the football team sitting close to us sort of make a shield around us with their bodies so that no one can see us smooching each other. And smooch each other we do, as Laurie and I kiss so much that my body seems like it is on fire, especially the one part that I think I could have hung a towel on. Or two. Or three. I have to shift positions two or three times so that my modock stump-like pecker won't be on display for any and all at the school to see. We don't stop our sweet lip friction until the pep rally is over, and we only figure that out when everyone else starts getting up to leave. I can't tell you one damn thing that happened during the last part of the pep rally, which makes it the best one that I've ever attended by far. And it gets even better when we leave the gym to go back to class. Steven and I have just walked out and are strolling back over to our fifth period study hall when I hear this familiar female voice yell, "Eddddddddddddddddddddd!" I turn around real quick, and there is Laurie. She gets right to the point.

"Ed Williams, I don't know about you, but I had a damn good time in that gym! My body is humming like a horny little old bee!"

I nod a little shyly, as people are streaming by us on their way back to class, and Laurie is talkin' real loud, so I'm just a tad embarrassed. Doesn't make a damn bit of difference to Laurie, though, based on what she says next.

"Baby, I don't know about you, but I didn't get enough. Do you want some more?"

Hell, I'm a Williams, as if she needed to ask me that at all, so I figure we're gonna make plans to go out on a date or something right there on the spot. I tell her that I want some more, and then I find out I'm wrong about what I think we're gonna do. We don't make plans for a date. Instead, Laurie walks right up to me, right in front of Steven and all those people who happen to be walking by, and gives me a kiss that is just about like a whale sucking the air out of a maypop. She damn near takes a portion of my face off as she's kissin' on me so deep and hard and good! It's great, but she just won't stop, and continues to kiss on me for another ten minutes or so.

I'm in one helluva quandary, to tell you the truth. On the one hand, all these people are walkin' by, and I am positive that a teacher might be soon among them. If a teacher sees me standing there in the parking lot with a blonde kissing on me like they do in one of those porno movies, then my ass is gonna be in detention until the day the Beav becomes a grandfather. Hell, I might even be taking a chance of fouling up my graduation over being involved in something like this. People at MP have been suspended for getting carried away a little too much with the opposite sex on school grounds before, and I don't want something like that on my permanent record. On the other hand, Mr. Happy is standing up again like one of those Howard Johnson's motel signs, and if Laurie suddenly stops kissing me and walks away, all those people going by will immediately notice that my mind is not on eleventh grade algebra. I guess my fear of being suspended wins out over my fear of being noticed toting some trouser wood, so I pull away from Laurie just a little.

She looks up into my eyes and says, "What's wrong, hungry baby?" I stammer back something about wanting a little more privacy, and she says, "Well baby, just have it however you want it." And with that, she leans forward, kisses me on the cheek, and walks off.

Steven is still standing there with me, although he looks a tad flushed, and we both laugh and make our way back to our study hall. He has some math stuff he needs to be working on, as Steven is enrolled in the most advanced math class Mary Persons offers, Algebra-Trig. When we get back to our room he works on math problems and I spend a lot of time looking out the window, mostly thinking about Laurie, and then thinking about sitting with Kim on the school bus ride home.

Oh, I forgot to tell ya'll about Kim. She's very pretty, and I've known her since she was a tiny little girl. She's about three years behind me in school, and I've noticed here lately that Kim has grown up quite a bit. She's pretty, smart, and I found out a couple of afternoons ago while riding home on the bus that she can really kiss good. It was funny—we were sitting there talking to each other, and I noticed we kept looking right into each other's eyes, like we were scouting each other out for pimples or something. Maybe a better way of explaining it is that we were looking into each other's eyes long enough to know that we both wanted more from each other than conversation. Finally, I sort of leaned forward, and she sort of leaned forward, and our lips touched, and then it got a bit more intense. And right then and there I learned that Kim was growing up big-time, and I sure liked it, so the past couple of days we've been sneaking in a smooch or two in the back of the bus whenever we can get away with it. I sure hope the same holds true today when we take the bus home in just a couple of hours.

Study hall finally ends, and sixth period happens to be Physical Education, which means an hour of weight training over at the gym. If you play football at Mary Persons you have to take P.E. for sixth period, and if it's the off-season that means you lift weights and run. We lift weights on Monday, Wednesday, and Friday, and we also have to run a mile-and-a-half on Tuesdays and Thursdays. I like the weight training much more than the running, 'cause we have to do all of our running on an old road that runs just behind the school, and it happens to be paved and also happens to be hotter than a four dollar whore. It's a miserable bitch to run on, as the black asphalt triple radiates the heat, and you'd be surprised at how much dust you can pick up from just off the side of the road while you are running. Nothing like gasping like hell for air and simultaneously sucking up quarts of red dust in your lungs as your legs get bathed in two hundred plus degree heat. All in all, it's almost enough to make you consider quitting football and becoming one of the band queers. Notice that I said *consider* becoming one—I have a dad who would put his foot in my ass up to the laces if I ever truly considered doing something like that.

Anyway, since today's Friday we lift weights. I have a decent workout. The only thing worth talkin' about is when Whiff Walker does his pull-ups. Coach Peavy is counting off his reps, and Whiff is straining to do them, almost like a constipated goose strains the grain. That's one thing I really like about Whiff—he goes as hard as he can go whenever he does something. Hell, if he takes a shit he tries to take the fastest and biggest one on the team. A true competitive shitter.

Anyway, getting back to what I was sayin', Whiff is doing his reps on the pull-up bar, Coach Peavy is standing right behind him, and Whiff is just about tuckered out. He tries to pull himself up that bar one more time and when he does, his face gets all red and his arms quiver and suddenly a Hiroshima-like fart blasts out of his ass and catches Coach Peavy right at point-blank range. I swear that he staggers back a step or two from the impact. The worst thing is that Whiff eats shit like baked beans and raisin bran all the time, so the fart itself is mega, mega rank. Needless to say, the rest of us almost bust out our stomachs from laughing, and then Audie Rooks praises Whiff for "...going for the long ball." Speaking for the rest of us, I think we're just thankful that we're standing close to a window fan that blows the fart out away from us. It really doesn't take that long for the room to get back to normal, except for Coach Peavy, who seems a bit rattled even after it happened, and who worries out loud that the fart would cling to his clothes and that he would be socially unacceptable for the rest of the day.

After showering, I run out and get on the bus, plopping down in one of the back seats. I'm mostly thinking about what Jenny and I are gonna do on our date later this evening, and while I'm doing that Kim walks up and plunks herself right down in my seat. God, she looks good. No, I take that back, she looks gooooodddd! Young, firm, big blue eyes, and lips that I think are the most kissable I've ever experienced. I really don't have any business foolin' around with her, but dammit, why does my mind tell me one thing and my dick tells me something totally different? It's like I'm at war with myself, the good and bad stuff dueling, but the ole pink crusader seems to win out almost every time.

Mr. R. L. Watkins cranks up the bus to begin our trip home, which means that I am now free to kiss Kim—I can't do it when we're sitting still because you never know when one of the other girls that I'm true lovin' might happen to walk by. If that happens, the shit'll hit the fan like machine gun bullets, and that's me being nice about it. I saw that for myself firsthand about four or five years ago. I was in the fifth or sixth grade, but I still knew what was goin' on when it comes to he-in' and she-in'. The gist of it was that one of the guys on the football team back at that time, Buzz Porch, rode on the same school bus that I did. He was goin' steady with this girl named Sheila, but the only problem was that ole' Buzz was about as true to her as a cash-strapped hooker. Anyway, as near as I can tell, Sheila had spied Buzz out on a date the evening before with someone other than her, some girl named Fran. I learned this to be the case when Sheila got on the bus the next morning. Normally, she's one of those people whose smile lights up the whole bus, but on this particular morning she looked like she had just gotten over one of those twenty-four hour viruses where all you do is lose everything through either your ass or your mouth. She was right close to being evil looking, and she walked right up to where Buzz was sittin' and sat down next to him. Ole' Buzz, I guess he figured he'd get him a little kissy, so he leaned over to get himself a quick one. When that happened, Sheila pulled back, and said real loud where the whole bus could hear, "Don't be puckering up your lips to kiss on me, Buzz Porch! Any man who would kiss a whore like Fran would probably nibble up on a rat's ass! Take your two-timin' hide off to some other seat, and be quick about it! You also might want to get Dr. Bramblett to go on ahead and give you a penicillin shot so that you'll be one step ahead of the game."

Most of us laughed like hell, which inspired ole Buzz to try to sweet talk his way out of it by saying the following: "Look Sheila, you and me had just had that fight a couple of days before, and Fran was bein' all sweet to me and all, and before I knew it she was huggin' and kissin' me! I didn't even know what to do about it because I was so surprised. But then I figured that a true gentleman doesn't just pull away from a lady who is expressing true kindness towards him. I had to kiss her right back just to be kind, but I thought about you the whole time I was doing it."

Personally, I couldn't believe that Buzz had the balls to even try some bullshit like that, and Sheila didn't buy into it herself because she hauled off and slapped him right across his face. The sound from it was so loud that it made my face sting. Then, she marched a few seats back and sat down right next to me because I had no one else sitting with me. Talk about one helluva situation to find yourself in—here I am, a fifth or sixth grader, sittin' with a girl who has just swatted the hell out of one of our star football players. She didn't say much to me, she simply sat down and started squalling like a virgin onion peeler. Me, I didn't know what to do. I sat there for awhile, looked out of the window, and then I turned back around towards her. She was all red-eyed and puffy-faced, and I knew that I had to say something to her, so I tried this, "I know I can't help you, but I sure wish I could." Man, I wish I hadn't of said it. Sheila gave me this real funny look, double clutched up on her squallin', and then gave me this really huge hug. Honest to God, she wrapped her arms around mine, sort of pinning my arms down by my sides, and hugged me like a bag of hot

Krystals in December. I mostly enjoyed it, to tell ya'll the truth, but then I got uncomfortable for a couple of good reasons:

1. Sheila was a girl, a damn pretty girl, and all that hugging made my personal love thermometer percolate like a pot of hot Irish coffee.

2. Even though I was just a little piss, a fifth or sixth grader at best, ole Buzz was giving me a somewhat menacing look. Sort of like one of those looks an alligator mama gives Marlin Perkins when he gets too close to her nest. I really didn't think that Buzz would whup a fifth or sixth grader's ass, but when women are involved and guys are horny, anything is possible.

Sheila finally unhugged me, and then ignored Buzz's apologies all the way to school. When the bus finally arrived and she got up to get off, she hugged me again and whispered that she wished I was older. That caused my middle leg to jump up like a kangaroo, but she left so quickly that I didn't even turn red or anything.

My mind snaps back to now when I hear Kim say, "Well, if whatever you're thinking about is more important than me, then let me go sit somewhere else." I damn sure don't want her to do that, so I reply, "Look, sweetie, the reason I was so distracted is that I was thinking about a place I want to take you."

Kim actually seems to buy into that, which surprises me as she is usually pretty savvy, but maybe God tossed me a much-needed favor on this one. It's a good thing, as these days I seem to need all the favors I can get. Anyway, she wants to know where I was thinking about taking her, so I say that I want to take her over to the drive-in one night to watch movies and do some smoochin'.

Kim lights up like a Christmas tree when I say that, so she says back to me, "Here's one for practice so that we'll be good at it when you take me to the drive-in."

With that, she leans over and kisses me so wetly and sweetly that I think all my toes will invert. I kiss her back with equivalent gusto, and it gets so good that we both start to do a little squeezing and groping. Nothing terribly bad, mind you, just a couple of things that we can easily get away with on the bus. It's really goin' good and then some, but I start thinkin' about what a kiss whore I'm becoming, having just kissed Laurie a few minutes earlier, and if I'm lucky and don't piss her off or something later this evening, Jenny. But, hell, maybe being a kiss whore isn't the worst thing in the world. Geez, it's not like being a haint, having armpit odor, or coming down with leprosy or something. Kiss whore or not, I'll just live with it, as no man with any lead in his pencil wouldn't want to keep on doin' what I'm doin'.

We both come up for air and discover that a lot of people on this bus are staring at us. We even get some applause from one or two of the hornier types, so I nod at them and smile. Kim, on the other hand, gets pretty mad, and tells one of them that they couldn't get laid if they had a million dollar bill tied around their dick. That sounds pretty profound to me, although when I really think closely about what she just said it makes me want to cross my legs very tightly.

Time flies by pretty quickly when you knock off one or two deep kisses, and soon it's time for Kim to get off the bus. Right before she leaves, she leans over and whispers to me that she would call me later on about when we could set up our date to the drive-in. I sort of wince when she says that, as my social calendar seems to be fuller than Kate Smith these days, but I quickly turn it into a smile and ask Kim to let me call her. She smiles back, tells me she looks forward to talking about the details of our future date, and gets off the bus. She even turns around and waves at me as she is walking up her driveway towards her house.

Needless to say, some of my comrades on the bus start ragging me out pretty big time about it, tossing around comments like, "Ed, if she smiles any bigger, we'll only be able to see her from her belly button on down."

Or, "Gee Ed, she does realize that she's only your bus babe?"

And the most sensitive comment of all, "Ed, if you got

off this bus and walked up that driveway, her drawers would be down before a snake could flick his tongue."

I laugh pretty hard at them all, the bus gets to moving again, and pretty soon it's pulling up in front of my house. I've got just enough time to suck down some dinner, change clothes, and then make my way over to Jenny's house, which is exactly what I do. Jenny lives in a very big house, an older two-story job with rooms that are bigger than the ones you see in today's newer homes. It has all sorts of moldings and stuff on it, and Jenny's mom and dad have done a good job of restoring the house back to its former glory. I always enjoy going there, so I quickly get out of my car and make my way up the front steps. I've barely knocked on the door when Jenny opens it, and God, God, God! She looks like a hundred million bucks. She has on some nice black slacks, and her violet sweater is enough to make my pecker want to ask the rest of me for forgiveness. I guess the reason why I'm so attracted to Jenny is the combination of things that she brings to the table—she's brighter than hell, and I really love talking with her about most anything. She's also very supportive, yet independent, and for some strange reason I love both of those qualities, too. Hell, I just love her all the way down to my heart. And when you add in how she looks in these violet sweaters and those flavored lip glosses that she uses, well, dammit, she makes my heart beat faster than the Road Runner scorches pavement.

I shake off the hypnotic trance that Jenny has me in as best I can, which is no small accomplishment. She tells me that she has a surprise for me tonight—a home cooked dinner for just the two of us, and then she suggests that we might go for a drive afterwards. I can already tell that this evening has potential success written all over it. I'm going to get to eat a great meal, and later on, get to smooch the sweetest set of lips in all of Forsyth to boot. I may be just an old scrub country boy from Juliette, but nights like this make me feel like the man who owns The Cloister.

I sit down at her table as quickly as politeness allows,

and Jenny brings out some roast beef, mashed potatoes, green beans, and a big tossed salad. God, the only thing that would be better than this spread would be unlimited Krispy Kremes and a big frosty glass of milk, but I wouldn't dare say that out loud right now. The food goes down smoother than a prom queen's thighs, and the two of us have a great time talking as we eat. Well, honestly, we don't talk a whole lot, as I focus on my eating just like I do my kissing, but what talking we do with each other is really good.

I help Jenny clean up when we finish, and then we decide to go out for a drive. Our first stop is over at the Dairy Queen, where I proceed to buy Jenny a little dessert. Jenny gets a small strawberry sundae, and I get a large hot fudge one with so much fudge on it that you almost can't find the ice cream. I've learned from past experience that whenever I eat a big sundae I get mega thirsty, so I get a glass of ice water to go along with it. As a result, I'm sitting here eating big bites of ice cream alternated with taking big swallows of cold water. Jenny, on the other hand, is eating her sundae very ladylike with tiny little bites and all, although she does start laughing when I get one of those headaches that just throb like hell on account of drinking and eating cold stuff too damned fast. Those kinds of headaches are like red bugs and ticks, they're both useless and annoying, but what are you gonna do? It's not like I invented them or anything.

Once all the sugar is history, we walk back out to the car. I let Jenny in on her side, I get in on mine, and then we gun her back out on the highway. If there was ever a point in the evening where the potential for a little parkin' might be realized, this was it, so I give Jenny the biggest smile I can work up and ask her if she wants to go do a little private meditating? She smiles, says that it might be a fairly decent idea, and smiles again. I know at that point what should happen next, and that's Jenny and me goin' parkin' over at the Ebenezer Methodist Church out on Dames Ferry Road.

Yeah, I said that right—I'm gonna take Jenny parkin' over at the church, Jenny's church, Ebenezer Methodist, which is right out on Dames Ferry Road. And yeah, I already know that some of ya'll will condemn me to rot in hell for even thinking about such a thing, but do give me a chance to do a little explainin', and maybe Ebenezer might not seem like such a bad place for us to park after all. Just remember, one man's brat can be another woman's baby, if ya'll get my drift.

First, whenever a guy takes a girl parkin', he has to take her someplace that's very private, a place where the girl can relax, and be certain that no matter what she does or doesn't do that no one will ever know about it. Well, no one but her and the guy she's with, and the girl automatically knows that the guy is gonna lie like hell about whatever they did anyway, and she also knows that she will set things straight later on. She also knows that more people will believe her story than the guy's, 'cause just about all guys lie when it comes to scorchin' a little muffin. Let's face it, if half the guys scored that claim they do, there would be more babies than gnats, and that's a frightening thought no matter how you look at it.

Second—and I'm gonna get this right out on the table—Jenny is truly a nice girl. The odds that I'm gonna score with her anytime soon are about ten thousand to one against, but one is better than zero. And I'm not gonna lie, I would go without food for a month if Jenny decided to let me exchange bodily fluids with her. So here's how I figure it for tonight—if Jenny happens to be real relaxed and calm while we park, and the moon is right, and I'm having the luckiest day of my life, I might have a one in a million of a chance of getting lucky. Okay, shit, I know that those are even worse odds than that ten thousand to one I just posted earlier, but I'm operating on smoke and mirrors here at best. Here's a big thing in my favor—what better place to park when you're with a girl that might be a little concerned about the purity of your motives than a church? And parked at one right close to Christmas on top of that? If her guard isn't down in this situation, it'll never be. Plus, if I do get lucky, we're at the perfect place to begin repenting for our sins afterwards. So, it's on to Ebenezer Methodist Church for the two of us.

I drive us over to Dames Ferry Road, and Jenny starts giggling, knowing where we're about to go. That's one thing I really like about her—she knows that she's not going to do anything with me when we park, but she still has enough of a sense of humor to laugh about where we're gonna park. And that's exactly what we do. I pull up in the driveway to the church, slip around a couple of trees and park exactly in the middle of the back part of the church. There's no way anyone from the road can see us, which is mega good 'cause if my mom finds out that I'm parking behind churches, I'm liable to have to start wearing dresses in the very near future. Tonight is really quiet, so I quickly kill the engine, take off my safety belt, and angle myself around in the car so that my head is in Jenny's lap.

Okay, okay, ya'll don't start thinking any kinky stuff out there. When Jenny and I talk in the car, I sort of put my legs in the back seat and my shoulders and head end up in front and in her lap. It's comfortable as hell, even though it sounds like something Houdini couldn't escape from, and I can look Jenny right in her pretty eyes when we talk to each other. So there.

Our conversation starts with us talkin' about the upcoming Christmas holidays, and that leads us into the church Christmas stuff that's coming up. I'm not dreadin' the church stuff too much this year 'cause I just flat-assed refused to be in the kids' presentation over at the Juliette Methodist Church. Over the years I've had to get up there every Christmas and read little stories or poems to everyone there, and it absolutely sucks. When the service is over it gets even worse—all the adults come up to you and pat you on the head, and don't even get me started about all the kisses you get from the women in the church. God's house or not, it's always the ugliest damn women in the church that want to hug and kiss all over you. Some of them would gag out even the heartiest buzzard, and the worst thing about it is all the most intense kisses come from a couple of old women who wear way too much perfume and who also have noticeable chin whiskers. If you hug either one of them, the reward is getting stabbed in the face with all these tiny stickers, and you end up toting a Mexican cathouse scent along with you for the next several hours. My mom even got a tad upset at one old sister a couple of years ago when she felt like the old gal had hugged on me for a bit too long. My mom needn't have worried about it, though, as this particular old gal could get buck-assed naked in San Quentin Prison, and still not have to worry about anything. My mom still didn't like it worth a damn, though.

Jenny laughs when I tell her why I won't be participating in the kid's presentation, and she says that they ought to make a rule that if a guy starts shaving, that he's exempt from the program from there on out. I totally agree with her, and then we slide into talking about Christmas stuff that's happened to our families in past years. Jenny tells me that last year her parents stayed up real late putting some Christmas gifts together for Ben and Laurie, her youngest brother and sister. Apparently, Laurie was getting some kind of dollhouse that required a bunch of assembly, and Ben was getting plastic soldiers that came with their own bases, helicopters and air strips. Well, it took both her parents hours to get it all set up. In fact, it was almost two o'clock in the morning when they were finally done. Christmas Eve wasn't particularly cold last year, but Jenny's parents did have a fire going in the fireplace the entire time, mostly for atmosphere, I suppose.

Needless to say, with all the assembly work that was going on, both of her parents got really hot, and because of that they cracked open their front door to let some air circulate around in the room. By the time they finished putting all that shit together they were so tired that they didn't even think to shut the door, they just went on up to bed. Well, later on that night the wind kicked up some. By the next morning the living room looked like Homer Chambliss' store on Tuesday's poker night. All of the Christmas cards that were stacked upright on the coffee table were blown off, and some of the ornaments were knocked off the tree and scattered all over the floor. Even the fake Rudolph that was standing underneath the Christmas tree found itself sitting under it, looking for all intents and purposes like it was about to take a dump. When morning finally came, Ben and Laurie ran into the room to get their presents, saw all the cards and ornaments that were scattered around, and were convinced that Santa had been there. Laurie was pretty excited about what she saw to be absolute proof that Santa had visited, but Ben sort of felt like Santa had stuck his ass up in their faces, since he'd left the room so messed up and all. "Mom, why do I have to pick up my mess but Santa can leave his?" was his question for Jenny's mom. Jenny says that she didn't have a really good answer for it, either.

We both laugh, and I take the opportunity to lean over and give Jenny a little smooch. She has to be the greatest kisser of all time, so anytime I can slip one away from her it's a true blessing. I even tell her after the smooch how thankful I am to get it, and Jenny laughs and says that I am in the perfect place to be giving thanks. I have to agree with her on that one, which starts me to thinking and then talking to her about a Christmas Eve experience we had at our house a few years ago. I think I was maybe eight years old at the time, which would've made Brother six. Anyway, we were going to bed on this particular Christmas Eve, which meant that we would've both had to be in bed around 9:00 pm. I can remember Brother and I both getting into our beds and literally hating to get up under the covers. I mean, let's face it—who could sleep on Christmas Eve? I can remember doing things like counting sheep, or even doing another little brain trick that always makes me go to sleep. I know it sounds crazy, but even now if I have trouble sleeping all I have to do is this simple thing and it will just about always cause me to nod right out. It involves just a simple scene that I play through my brain…

I'm out on a rainy road on a cool night, my car having just broken down. I happen to come upon an old house, an apparently abandoned one that is really, really huge, almost as big as a castle. I run up to it, just happier than hell to get my ass out of the rain. After listening and looking around some, I determine that no one is there, so I go on inside. After looking around in a couple of rooms, I hear a noise. Scared and unsure of what might be there in the house with me, I crawl up underneath a sofa and listen. Slowly but surely, I hear intermittent steps—huge, heavy-sounding steps. As they get closer and closer, I notice a figure coming into the room, and it's the Frankenstein monster! He's older than hell, and is just wandering aimlessly around the house. Once I get over my total surprise, I have a real choice to make—do I go back out into the rain and wander around getting soaked, or do I spend the night in the big house with Frankie? I always opt to take my chances with Frankie, and I figure that I increase my odds of successfully surviving the night by being totally still and quiet. And, for some unknown reason, whenever I do that, I relax, nod off, and go right to sleep.

Okay, it's weird and I'll admit it, but it puts me to sleep, dammit. And it also has gotten my dumb ass off the Christmas Eve story that I am tryin' to tell Jenny. Anyway, I tell her that Brother and I had gotten into bed this particular Christmas Eve around nine, and that we could not go to sleep for the life of us. I've talked to friends of mine about this, and they all were the same way—before we all discovered the truth about Christmas and Santa, Christmas Eve was absolutely the longest night of the year. All you can think about is getting your gifts, what you want, what you think you'll get, etc. And then you get to feeling guilty about just thinking about your gifts, so you start thinking about Jesus, how He died, and what He means to everyone now. And that makes you feel really good inside, so you start feeling peaceful. And the only thing about feeling peaceful is that it makes you feel really good, and when you feel really good, you start thinking about things that you'd like to do, and before you know it, you're thinking about all the good stuff that you're about to get for Christmas again! So, no matter how you cut it, Christmas Eve is the longest damn night of the year, and on this particular night, it had to be the longest one of all time.

God, I can remember how miserable I was that night,

tossing, turning, rolling over on either side, basically just doing anything I could to try to drop off to sleep. And, after what seemed like ten years, I finally did drop off. When I finally woke up, what seemed to be hours later, I felt very fresh and full of energy, sure that it could only be a few minutes at most before we both could get up and see what Santa brought us.

My euphoria grew even stronger when I heard Ed Jr. walking up the hallway towards our room. When he cracked the door open, I sat straight up in the bed and asked, "Dad, is it time to get up?"

He quickly replied, "Damn, son, it's nine-thirty at night. You have a shit load of sleeping left to do before you can see what ole Santa brought you."

Talk about me bein' despondent. But, thinking back, I think it might have actually helped me go back to sleep. The reality of it all, you see. Anyway, before I knew it, I was cutting Zzz's like a big ole fat beaver, and I continued cutting them until I heard the following sound up on the roof of our house, *"CLUMP!"*

It was so loud that it woke both Brother and I out of a very sound sleep. We both sat straight up in our beds, and then Brother whispered, "What was that?"

I got quiet for a second, and then only one possible answer came into my brain. A loud clump like that could only be made by something really, really big, and what really, really big something would be landing up on the roof of our house on Christmas Eve? It didn't take me very long to figure that one out—Santa and his reindeer had landed up on our very roof!

I had to take a monstro piss right then and there but, with Santa on the roof, I sort of overlooked it. I whispered to Brother, "Did you hear that?"

Brother whispered back, "Yeah, you don't suppose it's Santa in person, do you?"

I answered, "Who else could it be on top of a roof like ours on a cold winter night? Even Alice Yancey could figure that one out."

Since Alice Yancey was the town dumbass, my point

was made. Then, we both got really quiet, fearful that Santa would hear us jabbering and haul ass on account of it. Both of us strained to hear more noises, anything that would verify that Santa was actually climbing down our chimney. Brother softly commented that our chimney was small, which made him think that Santa might not be able to make it through. The no gifts possibility rattled me for just a second, but then I whispered back that Santa wouldn't want to have to load all that shit back up on his sleigh again, so our odds were better than we thought they were. Brother figured that I was makin' sense, so we both got real quiet again, fearful that we somehow might blow this whole deal. Santa was about our only shot at some real loot each year, and damned if we wanted to screw ourselves out of any of it. Funny thing is, I never remember seeing a clock during any of this, but I'll bet that it took Brother and I a good couple of hours afterwards to get back to sleep on account of all the adrenaline that was pouring through our systems.

The next morning finally came and we both got up, ran into the living room, and saw that we'd received a lot of nice stuff. While we were happily playing, I commented to Ed Jr. that we'd heard Santa up on the roof the night before.

"Damn, boy," he replied, "That big pine out front dropped a limb on the roof last night. Santy always parks his sleigh out by the weeping willow and then comes in through the front door."

Jenny starts laughing at that point, and she talks about how amazed she is that parents could even get their children to believe in Santa Claus. I like her logic just fine, but the way she says those words—so correctly, her lips all shiny and glossed up, well, all of a sudden I don't give a damn about Santa anymore, but I do give a mega damn about kissing Jenny. So, I do the caveman-like thing and lean up and smooch her while she's still talkin'. She even says a word or two against my lips right at the beginning of the smooch, but I try to kiss her so good that she'd forget what she's sayin'. And I do pretty good, if I do say so myself, because she gets into kissing me so much that Santa is forgotten. Thank God.

As I kiss Jenny I think a lot about how much I care about her. I love her, if the truth be known, I think more than any ten women put together. Sometimes I get so damned worked up over her that I want to say, "Jenny, let me love you. If you get pregnant, I'll marry you in ten seconds. Frankly, I intend on doing that one day anyway." The only problem is, if I say that to her, she'll just give me a lecture on how we're too young and have too many things yet to do in front of us, and she'll probably add that it's not responsible behavior. She's right, dammit, and I know she's right, but sometimes I just hate the hell out of all this "have to do" shit. Ya'll ever notice that when you have to do something that it always sucks? And when you "have to do" something, it always benefits someone else, never you? I think "having to do" something ranks right up there with patience, which is the sorriest excuse for a virtue that I've ever seen. You show me someone that's truly patient, and I'll show you someone whose only positive attribute is their ability to endure pain and disappointment. Patience and having to do something—twin soldiers on the battlefield of inner grief.

Sorry for the semi-warped philosophy lesson. I promise I'll get my ass back in gear. Jenny and I kiss a while longer, but I notice that it's getting close to midnight, and I'm gettin' a tad tired. I also figure there's no need to get the one-fingered pink love bandit all riled up and then not provide him with a bank to make a deposit in. I think I even surprise Jenny a tad by pulling back and suggesting that we go on home. That's probably not bad anyway, if Jenny truly realizes how much I care about her, she'd have control over me like Hitler did Germany. And I don't like being controlled, especially by someone who could do it as effectively as Jenny. Anyway, the long and short of it is that I take Jenny on home and then go straight back to my house.

I pull into our driveway at maybe 12:15 am, and immediately notice something odd. A light is on in the kitchen, which is never the case this late at our house. We must be the most sleep predictable people in the world, as we always go to bed no later than 11:00. I seldom stay awake even that long during football season because the practices and games wipe me out early every night during the school week.

I get out of the car and figure I'd better take a piss before I go inside. I do have one little problem, though, and that is the fact that my one-eyed love doctor is stiffer than a dead man, so getting him out of my britches is proving rather difficult. And I've gotta admit that even I get tickled when I try to take a whiz while my dick is hard. It's like having this rigid flesh-colored snake that's determined he's gonna climb up a tree, and you'd rather him crawl around down on the ground. The good news is that I'm able to successfully manage the piss. The angle it arches upwards through the air is quite impressive. In fact, I almost get it up to eye level. After wondering if there are any Piss Olympics that I might enter, I finish up and go inside. I'm a tad surprised when I open the door and see that Ed Jr. is still up, reading a magazine at our kitchen table with about ten plates of food spread out around him. It looks like he has taken every plate of food that Mama had in the refrigerator and put them out on the table. He motions me to sit down, which, of course, I do.

I reach over and grab a couple of pieces of fried chicken, and then a little potato salad. Looking over at his plate, I quickly notice a stack of food which almost makes his plate look like a tiny replica of Stone Mountain. Something isn't quite adding up about this whole deal, so I figure that the best thing to do is just straight out ask Ed Jr. why he was up so late. So I do. And he answers with the following:

"Al, I'm having a hard time goin' to sleep tonight. I went to sleep around eleven, but twenty or so minutes ago I heard some clumping type noises just outside of my bedroom window. I walked outside to see what it was, and it was that goddamned pony of R. L. Watkins."

"Pony?" I asks.

"Yeah, a pony. For some reason known only to God and other horses, R. L. got a pony for his kids a couple of weeks ago. Why in the hell you'd want an eatin' and shittin' machine like that at your home, I don't know, but R. L. decided he had to get one for some reason. The only problem is, they tie him up every night with some rope to a post that wouldn't hold a bean fart. Tonight's the third time he's gotten loose since they got him, and I've just about had enough of it."

I ask, "Well, what can you do about it?"

"Al, I'll tell you exactly what I can do. I can get my ass on up in the morning and go over to see R. L. to talk with him about this. I'll tell him what the hell is goin' on, but I'll be decent about it. Personally, I like R. L. He's a good man, so I owe it to him to speak my mind. The bottom line, though, is if that damn glue factory trainee clomps around in my yard again, his ass is gonna be so heavy from buckshot that Jumbo the Elephant will look small-assed by comparison."

"So you mean you're gonna go over there in the morning and tell R. L. that you're gonna shoot his pony?"

"Well, the only way that bastard will be shot is if he shows up here. If he respects the legal property lines, his ass will remain slick and smooth. R. L. knows that damn horse can't just run all over people's yards, shittin' and snortin' on any damned place he wants to. I don't like to kick up much of a ruckus because I'm usually low-keyed, but when a rogue horse like that runs into your yard and basically tells you to kiss his ass, well, it's time to give him some proper discipline. He has to learn to respect others' property, and that's exactly what I intend to teach him—some respect."

Isn't much more I can add to that. I figure the old man will live up to his word and let R. L. know that his horse is treadin' on some pretty thin ice. I also figure that it is best to just go on to bed and get some sleep, as all that talkin' and thinkin' and smoochin' with Jenny has wiped me out, but the old man has one last question to ask me before I leave the table.

"Say Al, you didn't hone the tulip tonight, did you?"

I answer, "Nope, old man, I was with Jenny and we have a good time just being together. She's pretty special."

"It's good she's special, son, but totin' around a hot

slab of hard pink beef is not my idea of a good time. You might ought to find some old gal whose legs are like the Golden Gate Bridge, wide, and real easy to drive through. Just my opinion, though."

Sometimes I wish the old man would come out of his shell and tell me what he really thinks about things. Well, whatever, I'm not thinking about anything else tonight. I'm tired and I need sleep, although if Jenny got in the sack with me I'm sure I could work up the strength to do a little more than just sleep…

Four

I think I told ya'll earlier about the Christmas services they have each year at the Methodist and Baptist churches. When I was little, I went to the Baptist ones, but after the choir leader humped and bumped with the choir lady we all switched over to the Methodist ones. To tell ya'll the truth, I'm glad we did it, as the Methodists have a lot of advantages over the Baptists. They swap out their preachers every couple of years, so if you get a real clunker you're not stuck with him for too long. Another good thing is that they vary their sermon topics from week to week to week. A couple of weeks ago Reverend Malkinski even touched on politics a little bit, which I personally enjoyed a great deal. I don't know what it is about politics that I like, but I do like them. I guess it's maybe because politicians are so full of bullshit that you have to like them, plus there's a lot of ceremony and pageantry about elective offices. I also like how they can smile at each other on TV and then cut each others' guts out in private. I think the only thing slipperier than a politician is a Shriners' convention whore, and there's no need to elaborate much more on that. I think ya'll get my drift, and if you don't, you need to scale back from this and start reading comic books or something. Maybe even drop on down to coloring books, if you are that truly driftless.

Anyway, the annual Christmas celebration is tonight, and it's one of the two big Christmas deals that we have here in Juliette. Well, it's the only one that people can admit to out in public and all, and you'll understand the whys behind that later on. The other celebration happens to be something that we can't talk about out in public 'cause it's a tad illegal, so we'll let it keep for now and talk about it further on into this. A whole lot further, 'cause if I get caught talkin' about it now my ass will get tanned to the point that I'll have the backside of a Kentucky Derby winner. We will get around to it, though.

Honestly, I loved these Christmas celebrations when I was little, but the older I've gotten the more they grate on me. When I was little my Aunt Virginia (Ed Jr. calls her "The Sleuth" because she's nosy as all hell) had me get up in front of the congregation each year and recite some little Christmas poem or story. I always hated to do that. It was like my balls jumped way up in my throat when I got up in front of all those people, but Aunt Virginia said that I had "good projection," and should do it because I did well in front of a crowd. It threw me off some when she said that, 'cause I misheard her and thought she'd just told me that I had a "good erection" in front of all those people. Needless to say, I blushed pretty hard and couldn't even look her straight in the face 'cause of the sheer awfulness of the thought. Fortunately, she isn't wrapped tight enough to have the foggiest idea as to what I thought she said, so she just kept rattling on about how good it would be if I got up there and did something. In the end, I always gave in to her and did the damn presentation.

Things aren't like that now, though. With football and women and all going for me I'm a helluva lot braver, so when she approached me a few weeks ago about doing something for this year's function I told her that I was too old to do it. That pissed her off some, but she soon zoomed in to recruit some other hapless victim. It happened to be another young guy, and I won't embarrass him by giving his name out here. If ya'll really think about it, all you ever see at these Christmas functions are old people and children, and I don't give a damn about having to get up there in front of any of them. Just occurred to me as I sit here talkin' to ya'll. I guess middle-aged people just like to get all the old geezers and screechers out of their hair for a couple of hours, so they just stay home while the Christmas program is being performed. If I'm not right about this, I think I ought to be, 'cause it does make a lot of sense.

I head on down to Ed Sr.'s store right after breakfast, because I want to be sure and have some chewing gum on me tonight at church. Jenny wouldn't dare smooch me out in front of anybody at church, but I might be able to work in a few on the trip over and back. Frankly, I get a lot more smooches from her after church, as I guess that she's as relieved as I am for it to be over with, although she'd never admit to that. Another thing in my favor is that she probably takes pity on me whenever she thinks about the fact that I've been all trussed up in nice clothes for an entire hour. Whatever the reason, her smooches are worth all the other inconveniences, so I need to be really sure that my breath is smellin' sweeter than a honeysuckle tonight. So to the store I go.

When I get there, Ed Sr. is in the back slicing up some hoop cheese for Mr. Easler, a good old man who is usually more pickled than the barrel that holds 'em. I don't usually like hoop cheese 'cause it's tougher than cheap stew beef, but it can be pretty good when it's melted into something like grits. The two of them are laughing like hell about something, and that something is probably either women and liquor, or liquor and women, or some other combination of the two. I probably don't need to emphasize this much more, they're just two old men who have their priorities straight.

Mr. Easler sees me up front rummaging through the drink box, and waves. He and Ed Sr. speak a few more words, and then he starts shuffling his way on out of the store. And I do mean shuffling, as Mr. Easler seems to be just about to lose his balance anytime you see him walkin' somewhere. Anyway, right before he leaves he turns around and says, "Give me two fingers, a piss and some lead. If I can't have those, I'm better off dead." Ed Sr. laughs like hell when he says it, but I'm still not sure just what it means. Whatever the case, Mr. Easler leaves the store right after his tender poem, so it leaves just me and Ed Sr. standing there.

It never stays silent in the old store very long, especially when the two of us are in there together, and this time is no different than any other. Ed Sr. and I sort of eyeball each other, and then he starts things off in his typically low-keyed way, "What the hell are you doin' in here so early, boy? Whatcha need? Something to eat, something to drink, or something to help you hone more tulips than a Dutchman in a greenhouse?"

I know not to act like I am stove up or the questioning will only get worse, so I laugh like hell and admit that I want some gum or peppermint or something that will make my breath smell "like a freshwater creek" at the Christmas thing tonight. Ed Sr. laughs, and then goes around the counter for a minute or two. When he returns, he walks over and drops a pack of gum and some jawbreaker peppermints into my hand. I thank him, and he tells me that he's giving me those so that I'd, "…have fun, and have a chance at smokin' some britches so hot that Satan would need a fan" tonight. I laugh and thank him again, then, after a little more horsing around I'm about to leave the store and go on home. Something a little bit unusual happens, though—right as I'm about to leave, the old man clears his throat and asks me to come back there to talk with him again, says that he has something he needs to mention to me. Sort of strikes me as a tad odd, but I always listen to Ed Sr., so I walk back towards him again.

Haven't even gotten halfway through the store when he looks at me and asks, "Boy, do you ever get anywhere around Wig's house?"

Now personally, I never go up in there where Wig lives, as his house is in the middle of the woods goin' out towards highway 87, and it's just covered up in bushes and briars. For some reason, though, I can sense that Ed Sr. had some good reason for asking me that, so I fudge the truth up just a tad and told him that I did get by Wig's every now and then when I was out riding my bike.

Ed Sr. nods, and then says, "I want you to do something

for me, boy."

"What's that, Granddaddy?"

"I knew it was gonna happen. We're clear into December, and that sorry-assed Wig hasn't brought my damned jumper cables back yet. He hasn't even mentioned 'em, the thievin' bastard, and his ugly ass sits out here on my store porch every day. They probably went to a pawn shop over in Forsyth just as soon as he cleared my driveway, if the truth be known. A damned set of jumper cables like that can cost nine or ten bucks, which isn't a fortune, but it's the principle of the thing. A man who would come to your house on Thanksgiving Day and take your jumper cables is a man who ought to feel duty bound to return them. What if God gets pissed about Wig being a thief on such a good holiday as Thanksgiving? He's liable to snatch up his colored ass and tie four knots in it before you can say, "I'll respect you in the mornin', baby."

I've gotta admit that I almost laugh out loud at that, but I manage to keep a straight face because the old man is so serious. Then, Ed Sr., my namesake, looks me right in the eye and says, "Boy, would you run up there to Wig's place and see if you can find out about my jumper cables? I'd be much obliged."

What am I gonna say? No way in hell would I ever turn Ed Sr. down, especially after he had given me all this free shit and all. There's nothing to do but get in the car and drive on back to the house. Obviously I'd have to do that anyway, but I especially have to do that now. The reason is that Wig lives on a tiny dirt road that's a good ways off our regular dirt road. There's no way I can drive our car up in there without tearing the bottom out of it, so I've gotta get on my bike and ride it on up to Wig's. With all that in mind, I tell my granddaddy goodbye, get in the car, and ride back up to the house. As soon as I pull into our garage, I get out, grab my bike, and am just gettin' on it when my mom hollers, "Son, where are you headin' on your bicycle?"

"Just gonna ride a tad, Mama. Got more energy than a

mosquito on a hotplate."

"Well, son, just get back as soon as you can. Remember the church Christmas program is tonight, so you'll need to take a bath and be all cleaned up before you go."

I guess I'm at the age where I hate being told shit like that, 'cause I know I have to take a bath and all, but I still nod back to her. Then I ride off, feeling a little guilty about not telling her where I'm going. I have to do that, though, 'cause my mama would never go along with me riding over to Wig's. First off, it's so grown up back there that there's no telling what kind of shit is lying out in wait in all that brush. Some people have claimed to have seen foxes and even bobcats out in these woods, and don't even get me started about snakes. We have an ass-load of snakes here in Georgia, all kinds of 'em, and I'm not smart enough to always be able to tell the poisonous ones from the non-poisonous ones. On account of that, my philosophy has always been to kill a snake first, then ID his species later. I know that sounds pretty bad, but a snake coming into my line of sight will make me piss four colors, and I can only hope that St. Peter won't turn out to be a big snake lover or anything.

Besides snakes, bobcats, and brush, there's another reason my mom doesn't want me to go back there. It's pretty well known that ole Wig has been known to nip a little moonshine every now and then, and I'm sure my mom doesn't want me to potentially slide any of the "devil's refreshments" down my tender young gullet. That would be one of the top three or four sins there is, if you go by what all of our preachers tell us. Funny thing, though, is that everyone I know of who has tried moonshine absolutely swears by it. They claim it'll unstop your nose, clean out your pores, and some even say that it will make your middle leg harder than a baby hickory nut. And a baby hickory nut is one of the hardest things there is, let me tell you, so that's saying something. Fortunately for me, I have no problems in the dick department. In fact, I can get hard watching Captain Kangaroo, which worries me sometimes, except I can say in my defense that my sausage only gets limber when the good Captain brings out some nice looking little old gal on his program. Anyway, I need to get my mind back on business, if I keep doin' all this thinkin' I won't make it over to Wig's, so, I'm stoppin' thinkin' and startin' pedaling.

I clear our driveway, coast on down the road into the bottom, and notice a bunch of tire treads on the far side of the big curve in the road, just below this huge-ass red mud hill/semi-mountain that I'm about to climb. It's odd, tire treads on this side of this road, it's almost like someone has been parkin' here for some reason. Could it be a drinker sneakin' in a little late night nip? Or is someone nippin' on something else, i.e., I wonder if it's someone who's making nightly dips into Lake Vagina? Whatever the case, I make myself a mental note to mention these tire tracks later to Ed Jr. so that he can check into it. If anyone can find out what's really goin' on, it's Ed Jr. He can figure out most things faster than a whore makes change.

Whatever the mystery is, though, it has to wait, as I have this damn red mud mountain that must be climbed. No sense in even trying to ride my bike up it as Godzilla himself couldn't work up the leg power to pedal his way over the top of this big hill. So, I get off my bike and walk it up, staying way over on the right-hand side. I have to do this as my uncle Frank drives the mail route around here, and he's a great guy, but he drives like a damned maniac. On a big hill like this, he'll be going so fast when he tops it that his Ford pick-up will literally clear the ground. I mean it—literally clear the ground. And, since anyone or anything in his path would be mashed flatter than Goldie Hawn's chest, it's best to stay way over on the far side of the road so that you never risk an unbecoming personal mashing. Dying in such a way would be a bitch—imagine a funeral in a situation like that. Of course your family and friends would all be mourning you, but I guarantee you that some of the people there would be fighting back smiles. And, in an odd sort of way, you really couldn't blame them. "Yeah, it's really sad about old Ed taking a truck to the chops. Helluva way to go. Of course, they couldn't put the body out for view as his upper torso now closely resembles the front end grill of a Ford truck. And those don't look too damn good on the truck itself, much less on Ed."

See what I mean? Hell, I'm smiling about it myself, to be honest. So, the gist of it is that there's nothing else to do but walk all the way up the hill on the far right-hand side, and that's exactly what I do.

When I reach the top, I'm puffing hard, so I stop and suck some much-needed air into my lungs. Then, I get back on my bike and try to take this little washed out gully over to Wig's. The only problem is that there's no way that I can keep my balance on all these little ruts and hills, so my ass gets quickly tossed off the bike and over into a big damn bed of fire ants. They swarm me faster than a Swede pops a hard, and the only thing that saves me is that I have the presence of mind to take off my shirt really quickly. That solves the fire ant problem, but then it hits me that my nipples are standin' out like two erasers on account of this cold air hitting them. Odd thing, I never like to think about my nipples, and I'd venture to say that no man with two balls ever does. Show me a man who thinks about his nipples and I'll show you a man that cares about what the trim color on his den drapes are.

I take my shirt and beat it against a scraggly pine tree, finally getting it to the point where most of the fire ants are gone. I then put it back on, which my nipples really like, and the rest of me appreciates as well. Next, I go over, pick up my bike, and proceed to walk it along the gully until I get to a rise—not a real hill, but a place where the dirt goes upwards about five or six feet. I push that damn bike right up over the top of it, and there, out about two hundred yards, stands Wig's house.

It's fairly hard to see it from two hundred yards away, but I can make out a few things. First, the house is an old wooden one that hasn't been painted in years, and it has three or four old junked cars out in its yard. I quickly figure that there is no chance that anyone is gonna mistake Wig's place for a Beverly Hills estate, so I clunk on out through the grass, weeds, and limbs to get a bit closer, to learn and see more.

More might not be the best word to use regarding Wig's house. When I get close enough to where I can see it really well, the best word to describe it is sad. The windows are painted over with blue paint so that the sun doesn't heat up the inside of the house too much in the summer. There are a couple of old metal chairs sitting out on the front porch, those pukey pine green colored ones that look old even on the day you buy them. The wood on the house is parched and old—I guarantee ya'll the house would drink paint if there were ever any applied. The house itself, though, is a barrel of laughs in comparison to the yard. I've never really seen a yard made up of only weeds, but this one has nothing else in it but. Dandelions wrap up the place, and those sticker-like things shaped like starfishes cover the ground. Ant hills are out in abundance, and I even see a hornets' nest up in an old oak tree that is about twenty yards off the south end of the house. I guess I can talk even more about the place, but I'm thinking ya'll get the general picture. Despite the sadness, the poverty, and even with all the depressing shit that exists on Wig's property, one positive thing about his house actually stands out…

Color—there is actually color shining brightly at Wig's house! I discover this when I first walk around to the back side, right out there for any and all to see were blues and greens and reds and purples and oranges, plus mixes of other colors that I can't quite describe for ya'll here. These colors exist on Wig's clothesline. He has a real long clothesline, so long that it runs between three trees instead of the usual two. Hanging from it are shirts, skirts, and underwear displaying some of the brightest colors that you'll ever imagine, with lots of scarves and bandanas to boot. One thing that looks a bit odd in the midst of it all are some clothes that could only be worn by a tiny girl, little dresses and blouses that stand out in sharp contrast to the large clothing items that snap around them in the breeze. These tiny children's clothes just do not fit into the depressing adult environment that cast its spell all over this place.

I look all over for Wig, desperately trying to come up with some sort of casual way to ask him about those damned jumper cables. It's sort of embarrassing to even have to ask him about them at all, but I am Ed number three, and we Eds look out for each other. Well, we do look out for each other within reason. Hey, I wouldn't fag out to some guy for him or thrust my head into a nasty toilet, but otherwise I'd do just about anything he asked me to.

Finding Wig turns out to be like finding Howard Hughes. I end up walking around his house three or four times and can find no sign of him anywhere. It gets to the point that I figure I'll just walk on back to my house and admit defeat, so I begin walking back towards the main road when I hear, "Mistah Ed, the young'un! What is you doin' comin 'over here to see ole Wig? Please come back so that I can be of enty assistance."

It's Wig himself, and he's sort of stumblin' around in his backyard. I turn back around and slowly walk over to where he is. When I get pretty close to him, he says, "Mistah Ed, it is a pleasure and den some to see you here. You doesn't visit here much, although I do sees yore grandpa at times. The Mistah Ed, yore father, comes here once in a while, too, to see ole Wig and to ask me bouts how the huntin' is over around my place. Yore dad and granddaddy are mighty good men. Men like that they don't make anymore. It is an honor having you here wit me."

I smile and nod, my brain dancing around all over the place trying to come up with something to say to him. The only thing I can think of is, "Wig, I'm really sort of tired, can we go sit down on your front steps or something?"

Wig looks at me like I'd just said some of the sweetest words in the world to him. He immediately runs over to his front porch, picks up one of those piss-awful pine green steel chairs, and brings it right over to where I am, right out there in the yard. I don't know what to say, and, as it turns out, I don't have to. Wig does all the talkin'.

"Mistah Ed, mebbe this chair will hep you git some good rest. I know how damned tiring it can be walkin' through that ditch with all that shit growed up in it. I gess I needs a fuckin' lawn mower—ummm, excuse me Mistah Ed, I didn't mean to say somethin' raw to you like dat."

I tell Wig to stop apologizing, I mean, he can cuss all he wants to, it's his house. Then, I figure if I get a little conversation going that maybe it might help both of us get more relaxed. If we both get more relaxed, it'll make it easier for me to ask him about those damned jumper cables, which is a really good thing. So, I ask him about fishing and hunting, you know, like how it's going for him these days and all. Wig looks real serious like each time I ask him a question, then he thinks on it really hard and answers it pretty thoroughly. Honestly, if you don't know any better, you'd think he is discussing something before the Supreme Court or something, he is that serious about it. I even try to get him to talk about something really wild like poontang or nasty farts, just to get a laugh out of him, but he still thinks really hard about them and answers me pretty seriously. It's sort of hard to deal with, to tell ya'll the truth.

About twenty good minutes of this goes a long way. Let's face it, Wig's colored and older than hell, and I'm a teenaged white boy coping with a steel-hard dick. I figure I better go ahead and make a stab at those damn jumper cables 'cause, after all, tonight is the Christmas deal over at the church and the clock is ticking. It'll take me a good hour to get cleaned up and all, so I get on up and walk over to this one old wreck of a car that appears to still be running, and stand next to it. Wig walks up beside me, so I figure that this is it, time to take the plunge, so I ask him, "Wig, what kind of car is this?"

Wig quickly replies, "It be a piece of shit car, Mistah Ed, it runs like a goose full of hickory nuts—rough."

I then say, "Wig, do you know what make it is?"

Wig responds again, "It be a damned old piece of shit Chevrolet, Mistah Ed. It be a rag car, but it gets me where's I needs to go."

I feel good that our conversation seems to be starting out so well, so I figure it might be good to ask Wig where all he drove it, as Wig is old and never has appeared to have a job, at least not as long as I've known him. So I ask Wig where all he drives it, and then the strangest thing happens.

Wig gets still, very still, when the question comes out of my mouth. He begins trying to answer me, but it's like the words won't come out. I guess I make it worse for him when I stare directly at him, not understanding what might be going on inside with him. The old colored man swallows hard, and then blinks his eyes. Then he blinks them again. I know something is badly wrong when I notice one tear curling its way down the side of his worn face…

"Mistah Ed," Wig stammers. "I's apologize for dis, I don't mean to bring down a fine young man such as you. The problems of a poor old man is not something I should be telling to someone so young and strong."

I stop Wig right there, tell him to quit apologizing, and then tell him that if something is wrong he should tell me, that I truly care and want to know. Wig replies that he is like the sole of a shoe, there are millions of them out there and I shouldn't waste my time worrying about just one. With that, I figure I might as well go ahead and take the plunge. I mention something to him about my granddad's jumper cables, just some bullshit about Ed Sr. having some trouble with his pick-up, that we'd taken a look and thought the battery was bad and that those jumper cables would keep his truck running 'til we could get the truck to Forsyth in a day or so. It's all pure lies, and I am not very proud of myself for telling them to Wig, and I'm sure not proud of what happens right after I do.

Old Wig takes a few steps away from me and sits down on an old tree stump. Then, he breaks down and cries. Right there in front of me.

I don't know what in the hell to do. It's about as awkward a situation as one could ever imagine or invent. Poor Wig just squalls, he wails and cries, and I don't have one damned clue about how to help him. It's absolutely terrible. I hate myself for making him cry, yet I really don't understand what I've done to cause such an intensely emotional reaction. I feel like I should do something, but I just can't figure out what that might be. Finally I figure, fuck it, go with your instincts, so I walk over to Wig and pat him on the back. Wig continues crying, but after a few minutes he finally calms down a little, and then he starts talking. And I listen to him just as hard as I can.

"Mistah Ed, you don't know how ashamed I is of myself, to be carrying on around you in dis way. I don't mean to be so weak, and I don't want to ruin yore day. And I will go and get dem jumper cables for de older Mistah Ed."

I can't quite explain this, and I might never be able to, but I just can't take those damn jumper cables from the old man. At least not right now. As he takes the first few steps towards his house to fetch them, I say, "Wig, look, I really have to go, I've enjoyed seeing you, but those damned jumper cables can wait awhile. Why don't you keep them? Come to think of it, my granddad can put a new battery in his truck anytime he needs to, so he doesn't have to have them back all that soon anyway."

Wig turns, nods softly, and looks right at me. In fact, it's almost like he is looking right into me. His lips tremble a little, and a few tears still work their way out of his eyes. I nod back in return, then walk away, somehow feeling like I had done the right thing, yet also wanting to kick myself in the ass for doing it. Jumper cables go for around eight or nine bucks apiece, and I know that I'm gonna have to personally replace those damned cables. Walking home in the cold with that thought in your mind is not the most pleasant experience in the world. Hell, I would just as soon have sucked the brains out of a tadpole than have to think it. On top of that, I trip over a limb on the way back and sink my knees deep into some Grade A, red Georgia clay. Sometimes I think that the state crop, the state flag, the state bird, and the state song ought to be something tied to red Georgia clay. We have enough of the shit to fill up India, and it's not worth a damn for anything. So, as I now walk into my yard a potential nine dollars in the hole and with two red knees that my mom is gonna raise hell about, I have to wonder why doing the right thing never seems to work out in your favor. Hell, maybe the crooks and politicians have it right, fuck others before thee or thyself gets fucked. Well, I've really got to go, it's hard to write when you are about to be the main helping of a course of filleted ass...

Five

God, shaving sucks in the purest kinda way! It's even worse than kissing an old maid aunt with chin whiskers! I'm trying to shave off some of my whiskers before I get dressed for the big Methodist Church Christmas shindig tonight, and it's a dose of pure pain, let me tell you. I hate shaving worse than most anything, I think, and there's a damn good reason for it.

Ed Jr. Yep, Ed Jr.'s the reason for it. Look, he's a cool dad and I love the hell out of him, but he has this damned thing about saving money on razor blades. I swear to God that he will use a razor until he has worn the damned thing right down to its plastic handle. Why his face doesn't look like a pepperoni pizza, I don't know, but he always appears nice and neatly shaven. For me, though, it's a horrible struggle to shave with these worn-down plastic bastards. I'm slicing up my face like B-grade horror movie, so much so that I'm semi-fascinated just gazing at my mutilated face here in the mirror. There are all these tiny little streams of blood running down it, which would be really cool if they weren't my own.

Piss poor razors or not, I still have to use 'em, cause with hair as black as mine, the whiskers show up even after I shave. I just cringe thinking about what my face will look like when I'm a real old bastard, say somewhere around forty or fifty years of age. There'll be all these wrinkles and lines and stuff, and then this dark black band which will run from one ear to the other all the way across the front of my face. I'll bet by then that I'll be running that razor from the bottom of my chin all the way up to the top of my eyeballs.

I finish shaving, knock out the other two S's and get dressed. I put on this neat blue, red, and white shirt that has a Napoleonic collar on it just like the Elvis jumpsuit collars. I'm pretty excited these days about the King, as he's now back out on the road again giving live concerts, and I would give one of my balls and any of my teachers in exchange for a couple of tickets to one. Even with some of the good rock bands we have now, Elvis is still the man by a mile or two. I really dig the fact that he's from the South. In fact, if you get right down to it, just about any music made that's worth half a piss comes from down here. All the good rock music does, all the good jazz or R&B music does, and even the best church music (which all comes out of the colored churches if we're truthful about it, at ours we try to see how damn boring we can render a song) comes from down here. We're pretty damned cool and have a lot going for us here in the South, even if those northern piss heads don't want to admit it sometimes.

I get in my car, drive over and pick up Jenny, and any religious feelings that I have within me vaporize when I first look at her. She has another one of those nice long-sleeved sweaters on that she looks like a million bucks in, and I want to start humping her almost immediately. I almost hate to kiss her, 'cause I know it will cause my pink love gauge to rise up like Frankenstein off the lab table, but she'd think something was wrong if I don't. It's an interesting thing—it's hard trying to act cool around a girl when your dick is moving around inside your pants like the snakes on Medusa's head, but I do manage to sort of turn to the side when I kiss her so that she won't notice the profound effect she's already having on me. Having dodged this potential embarrassment, I walk her on out to my car and we then head towards Juliette.

It's funny how differently men and women look at things. Jenny is goin' on about what this evening's Christmas service will be like, and how much the children there will enjoy it. As for me, I'm pondering her bra size, and wondering just how much trouble I would get into if I just come right out and tell her that I want her so badly that I could eat leaves. As a matter of fact, right this second my dick is so hard that a woman could chip a tooth on it, and this trip over to the church is somewhat agonizing because of it. I know I can't say anything to Jenny about my problem, as it's one thing to be horny, but it's another to be horny and thought of as a genuine pervert. Such is life, I suppose. I'm telling ya'll, though, I've got to find me a pure-T whore to be my secret girlfriend. Jenny is absolutely killing me, and I need relief. Bad.

We do finally get to the church and there are cars parked all over the place. Jenny gets out and starts wondering out loud if there will be any room inside for us to sit. Personally, I'm hoping we find that there's no room at all so that she and I can leave and go someplace to be alone. As that tender thought swirls around in my brain, we walk inside the church. When we do, most everyone turns around, and of course, right out there in front of everyone, my Aunt Virginia starts waving and hollering like I'm up on the flight deck of a naval carrier. After putting the whole damned church on alert that I'm there, she runs up and hugs me, which means that I've just received a damned good facial scraping from her chin whiskers. Honestly, I'd just as soon have someone pour hot Campbell's soup over my balls as have an old woman with agitated hormones rub herself all over me. The only good thing about it is that it deflates my pink love adder rather quickly, so I guess I should be grateful to her about that.

She then proceeds to ask me several embarrassing questions right out in front of everyone, but fortunately she quickly bores with that and goes on to pounce on another victim. I'm obviously pissed over it all, but Jenny is laughing like hell about it, enjoying the fact that I'd just gotten accosted by the old biddy. Sometimes I wonder how my aunt got to be a Williams, as most of them are cooler than hell. But I guess every family has a few wild cards, and that's a very kind description for my Aunt Virginia. Kinder than I want to be, frankly, but I do have Jenny sitting right here next to me so I hate to talk about someone being mentally constipated with her so close by.

This place is packed to the rafters and back, people are tucked into every nook and cranny, and Jenny and I are wedged into a row surrounded by people that we don't even know that well. The exception is sitting right in front of us, Miss Simulah Smith. Miss Simulah's family has lived in these parts for years, and they're a pretty unusual group. Her dad, Muster Smith, worked as a mill hand for years, yet he was always dressed up in a suit whenever he was out and about. When I asked Ed Jr. about this, he told me that Muster Smith's wife, Miss Nadine, was screwing Mr. Carden, the richest man over in Forsyth. Miss Nadine was Mr. Carden's secretary, and apparently she was providing him with more than just some good office services. Ed Jr. said that Muster Smith was so caught up in wanting to be a big shot that he'd worked it around in his head that since his wife was giving free pussy to Mr. Carden, then, by proxy, he was married to the woman of the richest man in Forsyth! Utilizing that logic, he figured he had a right to dress up and act like he was somebody in Juliette, which is exactly what he does.

Okay, okay, that's probably way more than any of ya'll wanted or needed to know. So, uh, it's these two people, a whore and a kook, that gave birth to Miss Simulah, who, as I just said, is sittin' right here in front of us. Miss Simulah herself has been married a couple of times, but none of them ever worked out. The first guy, Rob Douglas, left her because he thought she was, and this is a direct quote, "one crazy stove-up bitch." The second guy, Barry Geisel, loved a good bottle of gin much more than he did Miss Simulah, which, if you get a good look at her, you really can't blame him for.

I hate to have to even mention this next item to ya'll, as I hate talking about women who smell bad, but I would know that Miss Simulah was sittin' right in front of me even if I was blinder than Helen Keller. Miss Simulah is one of those folks who only takes a bath every couple of days, and thinks she can cover up the funk by using a lot of perfume and smelly bathtub shit. Honestly, on a hot July night during a revival she can pay off so badly that the flies won't even buzz around her. Ya'll might think I'm kiddin', but I'm shootin' straighter than Annie Oakley about this. She stinks like a dead frog in the hot August sun, and tonight, every time I inhale, I'm reminded of that fact.

I have to get some relief, so I try breathing only through my mouth so that I can't smell too much of Miss Simulah's hard-stinkin' funk. This works for about ten minutes, but then, right when the Christmas service starts, I hear Jenny mutter, "Oh God," and I totally forget about breathing through my mouth and take a deep drag of air right through my nostrils. And when I do, let me tell ya'll, I almost pass out. Someone has let one of the deepest, stinkiest, most heavily sulfur-laden farts that I've ever smelled in my life. It is so bad that it smells hot, which just about causes me to gag out right there in my pew, which is definitely saying something. Jenny is turning a light shade of blue, and I honestly think she's going to get up and walk out of the church. I try to console her as best I can, and she proceeds to give me this hurt like look that seems to say, "How could you do something like that right in front of me, Edward?"

Jesus, she thinks I did it! I've never been as embarrassed, and I try to defend myself right here on the spot. I guess I'm whispering my protests a tad too loudly, because Jenny whispers back, "Edward, whether you're innocent or not, you're embarrassing me far more by talking about it than just by letting me suffer through it in peace."

Man, I turn red, and figure at this point that I have nothing left to lose. I'm just about to try and talk with Jenny again when my next breath reveals another white-hot ass bomb! Whoever cranked off the first one has just launched another blistering ass monkey, this one much more terrible than the first. I could make references here to sulfur times ten, but let's just say that this has just become the worst fart that I've ever whiffed in my life. What makes it even more grotesque is the fact that it doesn't even smell human. It's almost like someone has toasted some plastic or something and mixed it in with a bunch of sulfur. It's truly putrid. And now, right here in my pew, it's just hit me as to who the culprit is, and what must be goin' on.

It has to be Miss Simulah. First off, Miss Simulah is the biggest eater of prunes that I've ever seen in my life. The biggest eater times ten. Miss Simulah eats them just for fun, not because she needs them or is irregular or anything, she just enjoys a damned prune. That alone gives you an idea as to how ratted out and messed up she is. I've been at Ed Sr.'s store and watched her come in and eat a whole box of prunes while she's standing there, and a whole box of 'em usually has forty or fifty prunes in it. I remember Ed Sr. mentioning just yesterday that Miss Simulah had made an early trip over to the store for, "…some cheese, some milk, and you know she's gonna eat enough goddamned prunes to keep three Congo apes regular!" Then he swore to me that she had polished off yet another box right there in front of him, talking about her trick knee the whole time she was chomping them all down.

Well, if you take that, then figure in around thirty-six hours for those prunes to ferment, well, you have the potential for a ripe crop of lethal farts. Also add in the fact that Miss Simulah has, in my opinion, about a two day anti-bath funk going, and you can just imagine a high intensity fart working its way through her old, rank drawers, filtering itself through her thick polyester skirt, and finally making its way on out into the atmosphere. God, any way you consider it, it would have to be an almost ungodly, unholy air destroyer, which is what I'm sitting here drafting through my nostrils right now.

I thought I was having a hard time fighting off the effects, but I'm sure not the only one who's noticing it. You can always tell when a real bad fart is floating around because it's like it pisses off just about everyone in the area it contaminates. I kid ya'll not, as I struggle to keep from gagging out loud, I turn and look around at some of the people sitting around us. Several of them look like they're mad, furrowing their eyebrows and looking feverishly around trying to determine just who's responsible for this ass-induced

Hiroshima. Others have that look that people get when they're having a hard time putting a crossword puzzle together, and still others look like they just want to stick their heads out the window and take a deep drag of clean air. In the end, though, what truly gives things away are the people sitting on each side of Miss Simulah. That's what tells me that her ass is guilty of this nauseating salvo.

Miss Evelyn B. White sits at her left, as nice a lady as you could ever meet. Her family has lived in these parts for years, and she teaches school over at Bank Stephens in Forsyth. She was married for a number of years, and her husband died just a couple of years ago in a freak car accident. From all accounts, he was out driving on an old dirt road that runs from Juliette on out close to highway 87, and then cut over towards Monticello. It's a long-ass dirt road, but very few people ever use it anymore. I guess the reason why is because it's so long that it doesn't get scraped as often as most of the other dirt roads around here do, so most of the time there are holes in it that a carp could swim around in. On account of that, most people avoid it, but those that do drive on it drive like it's the Indy 500. More than one accident has happened there, and Miss White's husband, Mr. Roy, had one of the weirdest ones ever. Oh hell, let's be honest, it was the weirdest one ever.

According to Mr. Roy's bereavement notice in the *Advertiser*, he was driving his truck on this road over close to where Crandall Stamps lives. It seems that he was pulling up a fairly decent-sized hill when something shiny caught his eye. Thinking that it might be something really unusual, he stopped his truck, put it in neutral, set the parking brake, and got out to see what it was. Now, ya'll have to understand that Mr. Roy always drove these huge ass Chevrolet pick-up trucks, trucks with King Kong-sized V-8 engines in 'em. I always knew when he was driving up towards our house 'cause you could hear his truck at least a good two miles away. It always sounded like a plane taking off, which Ed Jr. liked 'cause it alerted him that he was coming.

Don't get me wrong, my dad always thought that Mr.

Roy was a good man, and he liked him, but he also said that he had awful bad breath and that he scratched the left cheek of his ass all the time. He would say, "Honestly, son, if you didn't know better you would think that Roy gargled every day in a septic tank, and that the left cheek of his ass was made out of mosquitoes." That pretty much should tell ya'll just how bad it was. Whenever he came by, Ed Jr. would keep him outdoors so that his bad breath and ass scratchin' wouldn't get inside our house. I guess he figured that the open air and wind would sort of mute out his stink breath, and no one would give a damn about his ass scratchin' outside. Good sound logic, if you ask me.

I guess left ass cheeks and septic tanks aren't painting the most glamorous picture in the world of Mr. Roy, are they? I hate that, especially since he's dead and all, but the facts are the facts. Anyway, all any of us could figure is that Mr. Roy got out of his truck to walk over and see what the shiny object was, and as soon as he got out of his truck, a Camaro topped the hill going about one hundred miles an hour. From what the police report said, Mr. Roy was knocked a good thirty to forty yards in the air from the impact. Needless to say, the accident killed him deader than a hammer, and the only mystery surrounding it was why Mr. Roy wasn't able to hear the Camaro in time to get out of the way. My personal guess is that the loud engine on Mr. Roy's truck probably screwed up his ability to hear the sports car coming.

The sad irony of this whole episode was that the shiny object Mr. Roy lost his life over turned out to be an old chrome-plated cigarette lighter. Yep, one of those kind that you have to pour the fuel into it to make it light up, one of the older models with the click-snap top. Poor Mr. Roy—he got snuffed out by a cigarette lighter, and he never smoked a single damn cigarette in his life. Poor bastard. Fate can sure deal you a pretty dank hand sometimes, can't it?

Whatever hand it dealt to Mr. Roy, it has just now dealt Miss Evelyn another bad one by putting her next to the originator of this super-pungent fart. Poor Miss Evelyn, and now I have to point out poor Miss Annie Bell Goss. Miss Annie Bell happens to be sittin' to Miss Simulah's right. She's a tough old sister whose family has lived in these parts for God knows how many years. It's been whispered forever around here that Miss Annie Bell is a rug humper as she's never been married, but I really don't care much one way or the other. She's tough as nails, says exactly what she thinks, and is the first woman policeman we've ever had here in Monroe County. Even the baddest ass crooks in these parts give her a real wide berth, as she would just as soon whup your ass as say good morning to you. And she truly is capable of whuppin' a lot of guys' asses. Even Ed Jr. has said that you would have to really think hard before considerin' a scrap with her. For me though, I have nothing but good things to say about her. I guess that stems from one time a few months ago when I saw her in Forsyth on a Saturday afternoon. I simply walked up and said hello to her. She said hello right back, but I almost messed up as I was so itchy-dicked that I was gawkin' at her tits, which you can't help but do as hers are two large jugsters that look like they could supply enough milk for all of Connecticut. To my never-ending surprise, she looked me right in the eye and caught me staring at them. I felt so ashamed, getting that feeling you get where you feel like you have a fever and need to sneeze, all at the same time. Even though I was worried as all hell, Miss Annie Bell didn't appear to be too concerned at all. She simply smiled in a funny sort of way at me, and even leaned forward a little, which gave me a better view of her big, pink Himalayas. I was thrilled to no end about that, and since then she and I have gotten along just fine. I guess we have some sort of unspoken understanding between us, and that's good in a weird sort of way. Well, at least I hope we do, just as long as it doesn't progress from this stage on into her bedroom. I'd be afraid if it got that far and if I didn't really please her that I'd end up looking like Ali did right after the first Frazier-Ali fight.

You total these two women up, Miss Evelyn and Miss Annie Bell, and you have two solid women who don't back off from a whole lot. And they don't regarding this megaton fart that Miss Simulah has just put out. Miss Evelyn gets the ball rolling when she whispers loudly, "My goodness, someone needs to change their eating habits, I think we've been graced with the after-effects of someone who's enjoyed a lunch of Red Hots and baked beans." That is a shot aimed right at Miss Simulah, cause everyone knows she loves those damn cheap-ass red hot sausages (Ed Jr. said one time that she likes them because she never gets a helping of some true pink trouser sausage, but Mama came in before he could say much more about that) more than anyone around these here parts. Miss Simulah blushes a tad and looks away from Miss Evelyn, trying to act like she didn't hear what she'd said, and that's when she looks right into Miss Annie Bell's face. You can tell it sort of shakes Miss Simulah up to be looking right at Miss Annie Bell, and it gets even worse when Miss Annie Bell whispers, "Simulah, we are in the House of the Lord, and what I'm about to say isn't very Christian, but it needs to be said. I can put up with your body stink, even though I shouldn't have to, but when you blend in the fruit of your ass with it, why, it's just too damn much. You can either excuse yourself and go home, or else we can have a real set-too right here. I mean it. I'm not whiffing your ass pearls for the rest of this night, dearie."

It's hard to believe that Miss Annie Bell just comes right out and says that, but she does, and Miss Simulah shoots up out of her seat like a rocket. She then bustles down her pew, walks down the aisle and leaves the church, whispering something to the ushers about leaving her stove on at home. All of our suspicions that Miss Simulah is the church stinker proved to be correct as all of the funk and farts clear up right after she leaves. Miss Annie Bell notices it, too, 'cause she leans over to Miss Evelyn and says, "Eve, it may not have been the right thing to point out Simulah's problem, but maybe it will cause her to stand a bit closer to the washrag tonight." Miss Annie Bell nods in agreement, and then their conversation ends as Reverend Malkinski calls the service to order.

I know ya'll are expecting me to say that I am bored as all hell at the service, but it actually isn't too bad. Reverend Malkinski talks about how the birth of Jesus was the single most important event in the history of mankind, and you can't argue too much with that. He also talks about living a good life and about being a good example to your family and friends, and I guess I'm a fairly decent example of that while the sun's up, but at sunset I sort of turn into something different. Maybe I'm a tad like the Lon Chaney, Jr./Wolf Man situation, or the Dr. Jekyll and Mr. Hyde one. Rev Malkinski also talks about Christmas being a season for children, and that we should all do everything we possibly can to be good to them this time of year. He says if we do that they'll grow up associating positive things with Christmas, Christ, and the meaning of the holiday. He then reminds us all that there were some really poor people out in the world, children who would get nothing for Christmas and who might not even have decent clothes to wear or food to put inside their stomachs. Situations like that make my stomach knot up inside, because any man with two balls ought to be able to put some food on the table, and I can't stand to think about any small child suffering. This isn't masculine worth a shit to say, but it makes me cry down inside to my soul to think about any child hurting needlessly. Just the thought is wrenching, and it makes me want to kill an adult who would deliberately cause a child to suffer because that adult ought to be willing to do just about anything to help that child.

I have to make myself stop thinking anymore about that 'cause I will bust out crying in church, so I make myself focus back on what Reverend Malkinski is saying. That isn't the best idea in the world as the good Reverend is now telling us this lame-ass story about a Christmas a few years back where he bought his wife some glass sculpture-type things for their dining room table. Apparently, he liked the glass stuff, but Mrs. Malkinski obviously thought they looked like shit because she gave him some cock and bull story about how nice they were and then she told him she was going to sacrifice and donate them all to the Salvation Army so that some other less fortunate family could have a better Christmas. The whole crowd laughs pretty hard, Mrs. Malkinski blushes, and I whisper to Jenny that the Reverend Malkinski is a really good preacher. That he is, but the main reason I bring it up is so I can score some brownie points from Jenny for being so attentive during the sermon. Normally, during any sermon I'll think about most anything other than God—women are typically my first choice, then football, and if those two fail to keep my attention I just run some good old Elvis tunes through my head. Elvis is really doing good these days, he's doing some concerts out in Vegas and all, and there are rumors going around that he might head back out on the road again. I would give ten years of my life to be able to see him in person, but there's no way in hell he'll ever find his way to Juliette. Hell, if he found Macon it would truly be a blessing from God, although I wonder if God would consider blessings and rock and roll in His same thought process. I've gotta start thinking about something else, 'cause God might use me as a cue ball in a pool game with the devil if He starts paying attention to all this crazy-ass shit going on in my head.

Reverend Malkinski speaks a little more about Jesus and the Christmas season, and you can see all the small children in the congregation getting antsier and antsier. The reason for this is that each year our church draws names (kids only) and buys a gift for whosever name they pick. We have lots of kids in our church, so this year there is a big stack of gifts waiting for them up under the tree, and they're ready to tear into them. When the tension gets so bad that it seems like the whole church needs to burp, Reverend Malkinski says, "Wait just a second! I think I hear what? Are there some reindeer outside? Why in the world would any reindeer be here tonight?"

All the kids start oohing and aahing, and Reverend Malkinski walks over to a side door, opens it, and in walks ole Santa himself! Well, it's not really Santa, but it does happen to be my Uncle Dog who's sweating it out in the red and white suit. It's really pretty easy to tell who it is given the cheap-ass

Christmas outfit that they have "Santy" wearing. The britches are about eight sizes too big, the belt is made of the cheapest vinyl imaginable and keeps sliding all over Santa's gut, and the beard honestly looks like one of those thick old woven carpet rugs that you see on the floor in a doctor's office. I did notice that Santy has some real rosy cheeks tonight, but I have a feeling I know the true reason for them.

Santy has his bag over one shoulder and a walking stick clutched in his other hand. As he walks over to the church Christmas tree he turns to lower his bag to the floor. When he does, it causes his other hand to come around and *thwack* his walking stick right into the tree. It's a pretty solid shot, several ornaments are popped or knocked out into the crowd, and a couple of tree limbs are broken and left dangling off the tree. Santy slips up for a second and said "damn" right out loud, which causes almost everyone there to start laughing and buzzing around like a bunch of yard flies over at the Winn Dixie. The Reverend Malkinski is trying to cover it all up by saying "darn" two or three times, but nobody is buying his feeble attempt at a dodge. Ed Jr. is tickled as all hell with the way Santy has just expressed himself, but he has to hold in his laughter as my mom is staring at him like a condemned man does the clock during his final hour. Of course, his not being able to laugh forces Brother and I to share his fate, as we both know that we would tote the red ass if we slip up and laugh out loud. That's the worst thing to me about church, you have to hold stuff in sometimes when you'd really just love to let it all out. We can't do that though, because Ed Jr. told me one time that, "If men could do anything they wanted, the world would be nothing but farts, jism, sass talk, and women whose legs were spread wider than the Grand Canyon." He's pretty much hitting that one on the head, although we guys don't wanna admit it.

The laughter finally dies down, and Santy goes over and sits down on a big wooden chair and starts handing out presents. He reads off each child's name, and then that particular child comes up and receives their present. Most of the kids who come up are shy. They just get their gifts from Santy and walk back to their parents. One little girl, however, is different. Her name is Samantha Griffin and when her name is called out, she walks up and takes her gift from Santa. Then, instead of shying away or running off, she looks up at him and says, "Santa, I love you and God loves you. I didn't get anything for Christmas last year 'cause my daddy got the cancer and died. Thank you for being so good to me." If that isn't enough to tug at your heart, the little girl then holds her arms open for Santa to hug her. Santy does, and there aren't too many dry eyes in the congregation while the two of them embrace. The little girl then steps back, waves at Santa, and returns to her seat. With all due respect to the Reverend Malkinski, little Samantha probably did more to remind everyone of what the true Christmas spirit is all about than anything else presented during this evening. And then some.

It seems like it takes forever and a day, but finally every child receives their gift, the proof being the torn up wrapping paper and ribbons that decorate every pew in the church. The Reverend Malkinski leads everyone in a prayer of thanks, wishes everyone a Merry Christmas, and then tells us that we can all dig into the refreshments. As soon as he says that, you can almost hear every ass in the church pop out of their seats and race towards the Sunday School rooms out back, which is where our church socials are held.

I want to get back there as quickly as I can because Miss Lily just about always sends some cheese straws, and I think that I might willingly go to Hell if Satan would just promise me all the cheese straws I can eat. Hers are even better than most, 'cause she'll slip a little red pepper in them, which makes the cheese flavor stand out more, and then you get that little kick of pepper heat right as it slides down your gullet. They make your tongue want to salute, and I figure that if I can slip back there really quickly that I might be able to scarf down a few before it's too late.

I whisper to Jenny that we really need to get over to where the food is, and she gets on to me for being greedy and for not wanting to wait on all the women and children to get theirs first. I remind her that they will be out of food if we do that, and then she suggests something that is really, really cool. She says that we should just speak to a few people, mill around socially for a bit, and then slip out and go to some fast food joint in order to get some groceries. If you think about it, it makes a whole lot of sense, plus, if we go with that plan of attack there might actually be a chance that we might get to go parkin' somewhere later on so that I can get in more practice at making tents in my britches. With a quick nod of my head, we both go out into the main aisle of the church to begin the requisite bullshitting.

Remember that I just said that our plan is to talk to a few people and then quickly get the hell out? That would've worked out just fine had we not run into Albert Burke, a nice guy but the long windedest fucker in all of Juliette. Albert is a great person, works hard at his job at Bibb Mills, and can throw the shit out of a baseball. He is so good at baseball that he was actually signed right out of high school to a minor league contract with a Class D Cincinnati Reds farm club out in the Midwest somewhere. He only lasted half a season before an arm problem sidelined him, and the rumor going around about why he had an arm problem was that he threw too hard during a game one night and then spent the rest of the evening with this hot little blonde who happened to be the wife of the local police chief. Word had it that Albert and the chief's wife were up on the second floor of the chief's house playin' hide the pink pool stick when the chief unexpectedly came home. When the lustful couple heard him enter the house, Albert's only means of escape was to jump out of one of the bedroom windows. That's exactly what he did; the only problem being that when he made his jump he held onto the window sill and lowered himself over the side of the house as much as he could before letting himself drop onto the ground. Apparently, his arm was still tender from pitching earlier that evening, and holding onto the window like he did really strained it bad, so bad that Albert ultimately had to give up pitching. I guess that's why Albert married a stout old gal with black hair, big biceps, and an ass so wide that Ed Jr. says the Postal Service would have to assign it two zip codes. I figure Albert must've decided that he was going to forget about pretty, petite blondes for the rest of his life on account of what'd happened to him, so he went about as far opposite of that as he could. Poor bastard.

Poor bastard, good guy, or whatever, Albert is not the person that you want to run into if you're trying to make a quick getaway from here or anywhere else. What makes our situation even worse is that Jenny and I are doing really good, smiling and talking and acting like we want to hang around all night, yet all the while we're makin' good, steady progress towards the door. We are only two pews and three people away from freedom (we had even cleared the Reverend Malkinski), when these piss chilling words ring out, "Edward, where are you goin', boy? Doncha have time for yer old pally Albert, here?"

I can feel the disappointment bounce around in my stomach like a SuperBall—it's that damn Albert, and worse yet, his old lady, Madeline. Madeline, as I mentioned earlier, is a stocky, mannish looking, slightly mustached old gal with an ass big enough to hide a school bus behind. A friend of Ed Jr.'s, Tim Womack, said once that Madeline's ass was so big that the water in her toilet had to have whitecaps on it. I pretty much doubt that, but I'd bet money that if you went into the bathroom right after Madeline had squeezed the cheese that you'd have to call out the Coast Guard in order to clear out the fumes. She is one haint ugly old gal, and I'm not doing the word haint true justice in this particular instance.

Anyway, whether they happen to be super haints or long winded shits, both Madeline and Albert are standing right here in front of Jenny and I. At this point both of 'em decide to be horses' asses and make a real big deal out of asking us where we're going. You know, doin' stuff like asking shit real loud so that everyone takes notice of us. I decide not to say a damned word, I just look real serious at Albert and that wide-assed bitch and stare. Finally, after doing that for almost a minute, Albert says, "Gee, Ed, you aren't laughing at all. Are things okay? I'm not making you too mad on account of all this joshing, am I?"

I lean over and whisper, "Albert, Jenny doesn't feel like she ought to, and we've gotta get out of here. Do you get my drift? And now, since you've called attention to us leaving, Jenny is gonna be super embarrassed unless you can do something that really distracts everyone so that the two of us can slip out of here."

He actually buys it, which tells me to never underestimate just how stupid someone else can really be. Then Albert whispers over to me that he doesn't know what he can do that will draw everyone's attention from us and over to him. I desperately want to tell him that just being his usual stupid-assed self should do the trick, but this is Christmas, after all. Finally, an idea comes to me, so I whisper, "Albert, sing *Silent Night*."

"*Silent Night*?"

"Yeah, *Silent Night*. Start singing it real serious-like. It'll get everybody to focus on you, and then Jenny and I can slip out the back way."

"Edward, won't I look like the dumbest shit in all of Juliette if I just start singing a song right out in the middle of all these people?"

I show lots of restraint. "You might, Albert, but the only other thing that I know of that you can do which would distract all these people would be to pick your nose or fart out loud, and we've all already experienced all of that that we need to for one evening."

Albert nods his head, and then gets real still for a second. Suddenly, without pause or warning, he throws his head back and starts singing real loud, *"SIIILLLEEENNNTTT NIIIGGGHHHTTTT!"*

I mean it, he really does it right out in front of everyone. A couple of old blue-haired sisters that I don't know flinch and spill their eggnog, and several of the men look like they just froze up, I mean, they literally remind me of a movie where the projector locks up on one frame. They don't move for a few seconds, and then their jaws pretty well drop right open. Funny thing is, Albert seems to be enjoying all the attention he finds himself getting. He proceeds to look around the room, notes the reaction, and then throws his head back and sings the next line, *"HOOOLLLYYY NIIIGGGHHHTTT!"*

This time Albert sings so loud that everyone in the back of the church eating comes out to see what all the ruckus is about. With all the milling around and coming and going, Jenny and I grab our chance, slipping by several gawkers and make our way out of the front door of the church. Once we clear the building, we wind our way out through the cars and over to where mine is parked. I do the decent thing and hold open Jenny's door so that she can get in first. She gets in, and before I even get back around over to my side she unlocks my door for me, which is pretty cool any way you look at it. I get inside the car and slip the key into the ignition. Jenny figures that I'm about to crank up, but an inspiration hits me right there on the spot. I decide to just sit there, with my hands on the keys, and do nothing.

Jenny looks over at me and continues smiling. After about forty-five more seconds, she asks, "Aren't you going to crank up the car and leave?"

My reply? "Well, it's gonna cost you."

"Cost me? How?"

"I want you to kiss me like you've got an appointment with the electric chair in the next thirty minutes."

"Edward, why are you holding us up for that? You know that we kiss each other all the time."

I now go for the kill. "Jenny, I'm all dressed up, hot, and sticky. The least you can do is add that I smell of a lady's perfume to that list."

I'm not quite sure why it works, but it does, as Jenny and I kiss like two horny rabbits for about half a minute. I guess I kiss Jenny pretty hungrily because she pulls back just a tad at the end, and I think it was because she knows that I am fastly getting to the point of no return. As for me, I add toting a rock-hard dick to being all dressed up, hot, and sticky. Seeing that I'm not going to get what I need, I crank up the car, slip it into first gear, and work my way out of the church's parking lot and onto McCrackin Street Road.

I let the window down and allow some cool air to work its way into the car, which helps some—nothing like cold air to take the starch out of an agitated dick. It also gets me and Jenny back all cozy again, as she quickly gets cool and snuggles in against me to get warmer. We talk awhile about where we want to go, and, of course, my vote is to go parking. Jenny, on the other hand, says that she is dying for a Peanut Buster Parfait over at the Dairy Queen in Forsyth. I really can't holler too much about that, as we left the church so quickly that neither of us has eaten any food, so it's on to the Dairy Queen I go.

We get there pretty quickly, and I discover one of the advantages in visiting the Dairy Queen during cold weather—you don't have to wait in line very long. Jenny orders a Peanut Buster Parfait, and I order a double cheeseburger, some fries, and a lemon-lime Mr. Misty. It makes perfect sense to do that—I'm hungry, want some regular food, and I figure desert is already covered, as there's no way that Jenny can finish off a whole Peanut Buster Parfait all by herself. Hell, there's enough soft serve ice cream in one to patch up all the leaks in a second-hand trailer, and Jenny is not a big eater even on her best day. At least that's what I'd thought up to now, but, as I learn tonight, there's always an exception to every rule. Jenny not only eats all of her Peanut Buster Parfait, she even takes a couple of bites off my cheeseburger, and one hellacious drag off my Mr. Misty. I guess she sees the shocked look that I have on my face while she does all that, and she explains to me that she'd just gotten over a stomach virus and has not eaten solid food for the past several days. Since she is just shaking it off, she is India-level hungry. I assure her that it is all fine with me, and I actually feel a little better, seeing that Jenny can be just as big a glutton as I am sometimes. Okay, she's only done it this one time, and for a good reason, but dammit, sometimes you just have to rationalize shit out to make yourself feel better. Let me just enjoy this feeling, dammit, I'm havin' a pretty bad night.

As we sit there eating, Jenny tells me how her mother and father are doing, and then she tells me that there is a new fast food place coming to Forsyth. I ask her which one, and she says it is something called Nu-Way. I tell her that I've never heard of it, and she says that they are out of Macon and specialize in hot dogs. In fact, they have been making 'em there for almost sixty years. A hot dog place out of Macon, Georgia. Jenny goes on to explain that their hot dogs are about as red as Yosemite Sam's ass, and that they pile on this chili that's made up from a recipe brought over by some Greek immigrants who happened to be the founders of Nu-Way. Personally, red hot dogs sound pretty damned cheap to me, and I figure there's no way in hell that I'm ever gonna want to eat a Nu-Way hot dog. Jenny tells me that I should at least give 'em a chance, and when they get their restaurant up and going that she's gonna want me to take her there. I tell her that I will take her after it opens, 'cause I'm bad about sucking up to her in the hope that I'll slowly but surely get to peel off her drawers one day, but my heart isn't in it one damned bit. Red hot dogs? Greek chili? Sounds like something they would feed a con before they neon him out in the electric chair, but I guess a promise is a promise. I can only hope that one day Jenny realizes that the only thing harder than an Algebra II mid-term is my dick on account of her, but obviously I can't tell her that. I just hope she realizes it someday. A whorey old girlfriend is looking better and better these days, but I do love Jenny. Dammit, I really do.

From hot dogs, Jenny starts talking about Jesus and how lucky we are to have Him to fall back on when times get hard. When she says that, it hits me that I have to go back down to the store in the morning to talk to Ed Sr. about those damned jumper cables. Given how I think he'll react when I tell him I don't have them, I may really need Jesus to get me through all of the hollerin' and shit that will surely follow. I mean, he's my granddad and all, but sometimes he squeezes a penny 'til it hollers like a fox with his cardsack caught in a steel trap. I mean, we're talking about a damned eight or nine dollar pair of jumper cables here, but I guarantee you he will go on about them like someone has raided Fort Knox or something.

Thinking about this impending ass fry gets me sort of preoccupied, which Jenny takes to mean that I'm not paying attention to her opinions about Jesus, so she tells me that I should take her on home. I try like hell to convince her that I am in no way ignoring her, but she says that she can tell that my brain is way off someplace else, and on account of that it would be better if I just take her on home. She then adds that if I think I can be polite and listen to her in the future that I should call her and she'd consider going out with me again. *Consider* going out with me again. Shit, right now I'm wondering if I shouldn't just give up women and focus real hard on football or eating or something different. Least I always get pleasure out of those things. Seems like every time I get into some kind of discussion about Jesus I always come out on the short end of the stick. Why? Who the hell knows? Regardless of that, I still think Ed Sr. is gonna have a real case of the red-ass about those jumper cables tomorrow morning, and I have a feeling that I may really need Jesus, John, Paul, Moses, and a bunch of those other biblical guys to help get me out of this one. To tell ya'll the truth, if I was old enough to drink and smoke, I would damn sure be wearin' both vices out right about now.

Six

It's pretty bad when the first thing you see when you open your eyes in the morning is your own breath due to the fact that it's colder than a witch's tit *inside* your house. Our house is always real cold first thing in the morning during the winter, and to understand why you need to be familiar with Ed Jr.'s winter climate control theory. At night he turns off all the space heaters in the house, and we just go with our electric blankets for warmth. The blankets are great, they really keep you warm, but the house itself is colder than a witch's tit by morning. You really can see your breath and on top of that, the inside of our windows are usually wetter than a whore's panties at an August convention.

This particular morning I try to stay in bed for as long as possible when the alarm goes off, but I know I can't stall off getting up for long as I have a helluva lot of stuff to do today. Item number one on my list—I've gotta go down to the store to get some gas for a little event that I will be telling ya'll about later on. Well, actually it's item number two on my list. The only thing is, I'd rather talk about it as opposed to the real item one because ya'll already know what item one is on account of all the moaning and groaning that I just did about it in the last chapter.

Seeing as how nothing that sucks ever ends without it having to start, I roust my ass on up out of the bed. Talk about waking up fast! The only thing that could've more fully opened my eyes would've been if my balls had just been submerged in ice-cold water. Man, the floor is cold, the room is cold and my breath is almost as watery as a poked eye, so I decide to go on ahead and do what I need to do in the bathroom, and fast! As soon as I open the bedroom door to take the three steps necessary to get to the bathroom, I hear a very loud, *"THHHHHHRRRUUUMMMMPPPHHHHH!"*

It sounds like six bullfrogs dropped right on top of a bass drum. I sort of instinctively turn my head away from the sound to protect my nostrils, and then my brain catches up to the fact that Ed Jr. is in the bathroom. Well, it's more like this, God is he *ever* in the bathroom. In a big awful, stinky way is he in the bathroom. After the reverb on his fart dies down, I look towards him and say, "Daddy, what a helluva way to wake up this morning." He ponders what I'd said for just a moment, finishes applying his morning ration of Style hair spray to his quaff (the Juliette paintbrush), and replies, "Damn boy, you wouldn't have wanted me to keep that inside me, would you?" I guess I don't have the heart to tell him what I really want to, which would be, "Yep, keep it way up inside you." I simply smile and make my way on down the hall towards the kitchen and the warmth of its space heater. Mama is already in there making breakfast, so I have a little time to think about anything I want to. With that kind of freedom, my mind goes back to a recent episode of *Mutual of Omaha's Wild Kingdom*, the one where they were featuring some big snakes down in South America. That damned Marlin Perkins kept talkin' about how everything these big snakes did was based on instinct. Pure instinct. It really got me to thinking, if a big snake like that can get through life on just instinct, why can't we people do the same? Most of the time, it seems like the more thinking we do, the more trouble we get ourselves into. I decide, based upon that, that I'm going to try simply reacting to my environment for as long as I can and see what happens. Sort of turn myself into a human snake, if that makes any sense at all. Well, of course it doesn't make any sense, but I'm a country kid, and there's not shit to do in Juliette most days anyway, so I'm gonna be a human snake for awhile. Arrest me.

Ed Jr. soon makes his way into the kitchen, and advises me that I can now go use the crapper. I purge all human-like thoughts from my brain, and slowly walk back towards the bathroom. I draw in deep breaths of air, as I figure smell is a sense that a snake would largely rely upon. I also look around a lot, and I can't help but wonder what a human snake does if a rat suddenly runs across the floor. My snake persona would dictate that I should catch him, but the reality would be that I would probably do a vertical leap of two or three feet and mega stain my britches in the process.

It's funny how you can get mentally into doing something that doesn't make one damned bit of sense. A human snake? Geeeezzzzz, and the worst thing is that I'm admitting to ya'll that I'm actually doing this crazy-assed shit. I guess maybe one day I can chalk it all up to youthful hormones or whatever, but my ass is sure embarrassed about it right now. Anyway, back to my screwed up reptilian mental state, I'm thinking about snake shit so much as I walk down this hall that I even flick my tongue out once or twice. I wish I was lying, but I actually fucking do it. A couple of times is all I do it though, as the flicking ends quite suddenly when I hear the following words, "What in the hell are you doing, boy, trying to catch snowflakes inside the damned house?"

I jump upwards a good foot and nearly shit in my britches. It's Ed Jr., and he's looking at me like I've just put on a pink dress. Apparently, he figures that he needs to give his quaff yet one more coat of varnish, so he decides to go back in the bathroom and reacquaint himself with his can of Style. And ya'll now know the rest of this story. When this electric-like sizzle finally finishes coursing through my body, I spin around and ask him just what in the hell is he doing? His low-keyed reply is, "Well son, whatever it was, it doesn't seem near as interesting as what you're doing. What's the deal with you flicking your tongue out? You're not sleepwalking and thinking you're in bed with a bunch of cherry pies, are you?"

There's no way I'm going to even try and answer that. I flush about ten different shades of red, and that may be an understatement, but say absolutely nothing. Ed Jr. looks at me for a couple of moments, then shakes his head back and forth like a man who is wondering if the hospital had given him the correct baby or not. Whatever he figures, he turns and goes into the john. As for me, I figure the best thing to do is to lay low back in my room until he leaves for work.

With that thought in mind, I walk back toward my bedroom, crack the door open, and decide to get back in bed. Without a thought, I jump right back in under the covers. In theory my idea isn't all that bad, but I discover in practice that it pretty well sucks. It's like jumping into a pond full of popsicles, it's so cold! I guess with the house being so chilled it doesn't take to long for the bed to cool off, and being in it makes me shiver like an old breed sow. The only real upside is I'm now definitely awake, and determined to get this damn day over with as soon as possible.

I don't have to wait under those frozen ass covers too long—the old man fires off one more salvo of Style to his head and then leaves for work. As for me, I have to pretty well get done what I need to do in the bathroom fast, as time really is of the essence. I slip out from under the covers for the second time, rush in the bathroom and take care of the "three S's" before the proverbial cat can lick his ass. Then, I figure that since I'm gonna have to go to the store and perhaps face Ed Sr.'s wrath over his damned jumper cables that I'd better dress for success. What I mean is that I figure if I looked a tad in the holiday spirit that maybe the situation over Wig won't be quite as bad. I'm also hoping that maybe things aren't as awful as I'm making them out to be, that maybe I am way over-exaggerating just how Ed Sr. might take the loss of a set of jumper cables.

So, I throw on a black pair of jeans and a red corduroy shirt. To level with ya'll, I'd rather eat my dinner off a cat's ass than wear anything red, and that's got a lot to do with red being the color of those damned Georgia Bulldogs. Or maybe I should just refer to them as "dem dawgs." I have a lot of friends who like Georgia, but they make me want to vomit up sticks sometimes. They are always bragging about how damned good they are, and I get so damned tired of seeing all those red shirts and sweatshirts and jackets with Georgia logos on them. It's like being in a jungle full of red-assed apes, but at least the apes wouldn't call attention to themselves being apes. I guess, when you think about it, the worst thing about being a Georgia fan is that you have to keep on being one, sort of like the way it is when you join the Church of God or get a tattoo.

When I arrive at the store no one is using the gas pumps, so I'm able to pull right up and get to them. I can tell it's getting close to Christmas because the price of a gallon of gas is thirty-four cents, which is highway robbery any way you happen to look at it. Those damn oil industry jack-offs must just live for these holidays so they can ream all us drivers out with these ridiculous prices. It's a damned shame someone can't come up with a car that runs on kudzu, 'cause we have enough of it around here to keep a car going until you decide to French kiss a jellyfish. It's really not good for a damned thing. Then again, lots of things that I can think of fit under that particular job description.

I finish pumping my gas, cap the tank, and walk on into the store. At first I don't see anybody in there, but then some men's voices ring out together in laughter, so I just follow the sounds on into the back of the store. There, gathered around the countertop that the cash register sits on, is Ed Sr., my Uncle Franklin—also called Uncle Jew—and Frank Blount, an old colored man that's been a friend of my family's for years. They are all huddled up together talking about something, and when my footsteps get loud enough for them to hear me, they all look up like someone has just announced a raffle for a new dick or something. When they all see it's me, Ed Sr. says, "Boy, we're working on one of the greatest mysteries of all time. Something people have pondered for years, and the three of us have decided that we're going to figure it out right now." Obviously, with a lead-in like that I want to know more, so I ask, "Wow, what kind of mystery, Granddaddy?" He thinks for a second, smiles, props himself up on the counter, and answers, "We're trying to figure up the numbers on just how much tulip honin' goes on in China on any given day."

I stop dead in my tracks, amazed at his answer. "You mean…"

He interrupts me before I can even finish my sentence, "Yeah, boy, we got to talkin' about it this mornin'. Just think about it—China is the biggest country in the world, and it has more gooks in it than anyplace on earth. The undisputed gook capital of the world, in fact. From everything you hear there are millions and billions of them rice snappers runnin' around over there. Think about that for a second. No one really knows just how many of 'em there are over there because there is no way anybody could count them all. No way in hell. And who would want to go over and try counting them anyway? Still, though, there's no harm in wanting to know, so me and Jew and Frank have got us a pad of paper here and are workin' up the numbers. I think we'll get pretty damn close to the truth, boy."

I'm still sorta floored by the whole concept, so I just go on ahead and ask him why they need to know how much tulip honin' is goin' on in China? Ed Sr. gives me the down and true skinny, "Boy, why did Columbus want to take a chance and sail across a big-ass pile of water not even knowing what might be on the other side, or hell, even if there was another side? Back then they thought the world was flatter than your Aunt Tippie's chest. He did it because, well, he had to know. He was thirsty for that knowledge, so he went out and got it. Well, if you look at it in that light, there are all sorts of things that people have really wanted to know about. Stuff like is there really an Atlantis, does the Loch Ness Monster exist, or who was Jack the Ripper? You see what exactly I'm drivin' at? And the one thing lots of people all over the world want to know, and the three of us are among them, is just how much tulip honin' is goin' on over in China!"

There's no way you can dispute that logic, as he is making sense in a sorta perverted kind of way. I figure that I might as well get into the spirit of things, so I ask, "Granddaddy, tell me more about why people are so interested in how much fuckin' is goin' on in China? I've never even thought about it 'til now, to tell you the truth."

"Boy, some things are just damned awesome to think about. Things like Niagara Falls, with that big rush of water splashin' out over the side of that cliff and fallin' down into the valley below. You know, there's not very much up north that's really pretty, but Niagara Falls is, so lots of people visit it each year and because of that they start wonderin' all kinds of shit about it. It's just how people are, you know? We're curious, and one of the things that gets wondered about the most is just how much water is spilling out over those cliffs. People don't need to know that—they just want to know it. They have this big-assed curiosity about it, you see. And they have that exact same curiosity when they see a big ant hill and wonder how many ants are pissing around deep down inside it. That's how the term "piss ant" came to be, 'cause of people's need to know more about those ants. Didn't know that, did you, boy?"

One never knows where a clear ray of knowledge will spring from, I guess. I shake my head, Ed Sr. seems pleased, and he continues on with his lesson about the major leagues of tulip honing, China.

"Well, that's the deal with the Chinese. There are millions, hell, probably billions of 'em livin' over there. I wouldn't be a damned bit surprised if they didn't have to stack 'em all up like cord wood each night just so that all of 'em will have enough room to sleep. Well, if you wonder about how many of them there are, then that exact same curiosity just naturally extends on over to other things that they do, like how much could all of 'em eat in a day, and, of course, exactly how much of that "filet-ala-poo-tay" do all of 'em like to get each day? It's perfectly normal to wonder about nature oriented stuff like that."

Honestly, I don't know what to say. Turns out that I don't need to, as he continues, "Son, I'll be right with you, just as soon as we work up these figures. We're awful damned close to figurin' out one of life's all-time great mysteries. Hell, when we get these numbers done we may send 'em on in to the

National Geographic or something because it's the kind of information they like to see. Hell, they may even want to do a big article about this once they get a load of these numbers."

With that, Ed Sr. turns to my Uncle Jew and says, "Franklin, tell me again, how many Chinese do you figure there are over there?"

My uncle folds his arms, furrows his brow, and thinks real hard over the question. I honestly think he may have thought on it for a good thirty to forty-five seconds. Finally, after some intense mental gymnastics, he says, "Daddy, just to make it easy, let's say there are a billion of them Chinamen over there. Hell, there's probably a lot more, but they're probably tucked away into so many nooks and crannies that no one but God Himself could ever get an accurate count. A billion is a nice round number, and we're probably playin' it on the conservative side. Daddy, what do you and Mr. Blount think about it?"

Mr. Blount just looks over at my uncle, nods, and grunts just a tad. Seems to be a pretty positive-type grunt, though. My granddaddy also nods, and then says that it seems to be a reasonable number and that any sane person would go along with it. And with that, he writes out the number 1,000,000,000 on a sheet of paper.

Then, he looks up, and asks, "Now, how many times, on average, do ya'll think that the average Chinaman hones the tulip? I mean, how many times does he hone one each day? And look, before ya'll say anything, just know that all the evidence is on the side of the fact that there has to be some heavy fuckin' goin' on over in China. There has to be. With a billion people, hell, the logic would follow that a lot of yellow dicks are being wiggled and jiggled each and every day. So, ya'll factor all that in, and then tell me just how many times a day do we think our yellow brethren are gettin' their rocks off?"

My Uncle Franklin jumps in and says that he feels like the Chinese handle sex just as routinely as they handle all the other normal everyday stuff that they do, stuff like brushing their teeth, eating, or taking a crap. "Daddy," he says, "I'm bettin' that they knock off a little first thing each morning, just to get 'em through the day, and then they cut 'em a little slice before they go off to sleep because they can't get stuff like sleeping pills or liquor to help them rest if they need it. They have to rely strictly on the poon."

Mr. Blount nods and says that twice a day made perfect sense to him, and Ed Sr. feels like it was a good number as well. As he puts it, "You know, some of the younger ones are probably doin' some super high intensity fuckin,' maybe several times a day, but you have to balance that off with all the old people and 'sweet boys'. Two times a day is a right fair figure in my estimation, boy."

With a good daily average now picked, they take the one billion figure, multiply it by two, and then multiply that by three hundred and sixty five days. When you do all that you come up with seven hundred thirty billion individual instances of Chinese wang-bangin' each year. Ed Sr. reads the number out loud, and it draws a big chorus of "oohs" and "aahs," including a few from me.

Mr. Blount remarks, "Any way you cut it, dat be a whole lot of cuing up the old hard love stick, don't it Mister Ed?"

My granddad nods, and then says he is glad that the three of them have the moxie to figure out an important number like that. They're just starting to talk about what national publications to send this vital information to when a car pulls up out in front at the gas tanks. My Uncle Franklin runs out to pump the gas, and then Mr. Blount tells my granddad that all that talk about tulip honin' has made him "want to cut me a big, sweet slice of that ole puddin' pie," so he quickly excuses himself and leaves. And that leaves just Ed Sr. and me, all alone in the store, one on one. At first, we just keep marveling about all the Far East fuckin' goin' on over in China, and then I make the stupid-assed mistake of saying something about wishing that I could jump on some sweet young thing right that minute. And when I say the word "jump," you can almost see the light flash on in Ed Sr.'s brain. He looks me dead in the eyes, and asks, "Boy, did you manage to get my damned jumper cables back from that thievin' bastard Wig?"

I don't know what to say, he's so direct about it and all, so I stammer for a few seconds, trying to come up with something that would answer his question but not let the whole damned truth get out. I figure if Ed Sr. finds out that I had a chance to get those jumper cables and didn't that he'd be madder than a preacher holdin' services at a debtor's convention. As it turns out, I am pretty damned close to bein' right as he figures that my reluctance to say anything means that Wig has stolen the cables and he would not be giving them back. With that firmly in mind, he starts lettin' his opinion of Wig fly around the store like shit through a goose, sayin' stuff like, "Dammit to hell, I knew it, I just knew that jigaboo pygmy wasn't gonna bring me my damned jumper cables back. I damn sure knew it. Why would I expect anything different from his sorry ass? He's been a shiftless sonofabitch in the past, he's a shiftless sonofabitch today, and he'll be a shiftless sonofabitch when they drop his ass in a six foot hole one day."

I know this isn't being fair to Wig at all, so I figure it's time to belly up to the bar and tell my granddaddy the truth. So, I steady myself, clear my throat and say, "Granddaddy, I know I'm about to step in some knee-deep shit with you, but the truth is that Wig offered me those jumper cables back and I didn't take them. Just didn't have the heart to."

With that, I figure the only thing left for me to do is to pay him for the cables, so I take out the ten dollar bill that I was saving for my next date with Jenny and lay it on the counter, right where Ed Sr. can see it. Then I tell him that this whole thing is my fault, and I should be the one paying him back for those jumper cables.

Ed Sr. looks at the money, then at me, and says, "Son, what you're trying to do for that slack ass Wig is commendable. You're a good boy, you're showing a lot of class, and it's obvious why your last name is Williams. The only thing is, you know and I know that Wig has taken these damn cables and made off with them. Probably hocked them for two bucks which he then turned into a bottle of old Scotch wine. You want to know why this is pissing me off so much, boy, why a cheap-ass pair of jumper cables is getting on my nerves so bad?"

I have wondered more than once about it. I mean, let's face it, being out of a pair of jumper cables is not like losing your whole Elvis album collection or something. I just look back at him and tell him I don't know, and that I want him to tell me. And sure enough, he does, "Son, one thing that I believe in is taking care of my family and friends. A man that doesn't do right by his family and friends is one shiftless bastard, someone that's even worse than a fag with hemorrhoids, if you get my drift. It shows up even more this time of year, with Christmas comin' up and all. Know how you hear all this endless talk about peace and goodwill right here at Christmas? Well, all that means is that people should be good to each other, they should care about each other, and they should live up to the commitments that they make. That's very important, because when you give your word to someone to do something, you're putting the Williams name right on the table, and that means something. It means a helluva lot. So to me, I look at Wig, a man who sits his ass out here on my store porch day after day after day and doesn't do much else. I talk to him, give him a place to go to ever' day, hell, I even slip his sorry ass drinks and snacks sometimes. I'm very good to Wig, even though I don't have to be, because I'm trying to do the right thing, and goddammit, I expect the right thing to be done by me. That's what's really pissing me off about this whole deal, that I've been good to Wig, damn good to Wig, and the thanks I get from that shiftless whore sniffer is a stolen set of jumper cables that he took from me on Thanksgiving and has continued to fuck me out of right here at Christmas. A man that would do something like that is the kind of man who would sell his mama's drawers for a dime."

Geez, you sort of don't know what to say after you hear

something like that, you know? I do know that it makes me feel even worse, 'cause Wig is really not to blame for this whole deal, so I figure I better try to do the right thing by him one more time. I look at Ed Sr. with the most serious look that I can manage, and say, "Granddaddy, Wig really did offer to give me those cables back. If anybody is at fault here it's me, and I wish you'd just let me pay for them and then we can be all done with all this."

His response is direct, but not what I thought it'd be.

"Son, you're a good boy, but I also know a shiftless, thievin' coal ass darkie when I see one. And I see one in that damn Wig."

Sometimes all you can do is say what you feel, so I do, I say, "Granddaddy, I know I can't make you believe something that you don't want to believe, but I do know that Jesus forgave a whole lot of people and we're about to celebrate His birthday in a few days. Maybe He would forgive Wig if He were here right now."

I can't even believe that I say that, it's almost like some stranger has stepped inside me and spit those words out. Whatever possesses me to say them, it does do one thing that I'd never seen before—it pretty much stopped my granddaddy from talkin'. He just stands there quietly for a moment, looks out the side window a time or two, and then tells me that I'd better get on about my business. Believe me, he doesn't have to tell me that twice, I get my ass on out of there and head straight for the house.

Now, I guess I can't put this off anymore. This is the point where I need to tell ya'll what else I have on the agenda to do today. If I remember correctly, I think I referred to it earlier on as "item 2", and maybe a few of you out there are wonderin' just what "item 2" is. Well, I don't know how some of you proper folks who read this might look at it, and I really don't know how some of you improper folks might look at it, either, but "item 2" is the other big event of the Juliette Christmas season. The event that I'm gettin' ready to go to tonight in a few hours. What I'm talkin' about is our annual

Juliette Christmas Cock Fight.

Yeah, we have an annual cock fight right before Christmas. Don't get me wrong, it's not a formal event or anything, there's no write-ups in the *Advertiser* about it, I just call it the annual Juliette Christmas Cock Fight because that's basically what it is. And maybe I need to explain just a little bit about cock fightin' to ya'll first, and then you might understand what's goin' on just a little bit better. Some of ya'll may not like it, though.

A cock fight like the kind I'm talkin' about is sort of like a sport, some even call it a gentlemen's sport, and I think cock-fighting originally got started somewhere over in China or Japan or wherever. Some place where rice is plentiful. Least that's what Uncle Dog told me. Cock fightin' involves roosters, you know—male chickens. Male chickens will naturally fight each other, so cock fightin' takes advantage of that particular fact and sort of adds on to it.

In a cock fight, you have a ring in which the cocks fight. It's called "the pit." Sometimes the pit will be a round concrete wall that the cocks are put inside, sometimes it can be made of wood, tires, or it can even be something as simple as a circle drawn in the sand. Like I just said, it's where the fight itself actually takes place.

Next, you have to understand that fightin' cocks strike each other either by peckin' or by using the natural spurs on their legs. Think about it, have ya'll ever actually looked very closely at a chicken's legs? Hell, I don't think so, let's face it, most of us haven't. For those of us who have, on a cock's legs, about an inch or so up above their feet on the backside is a little spur that points almost straight out. Roosters use these natural spurs to strike at each other whenever they decide to fight. What happens in cockfightin' is that steel spurs, called gaffs, are attached to these natural spurs. A gaff is a long, sharpened piece of steel that's usually about two or three inches long, and it has a leather stocking that's slipped around the rooster's leg and then tied firmly to it. It sort of reminds you of a leather shoe with a sword sticking out of the back of it. Gaffs are tied onto both fightin' cocks legs, and then they're ready to show everyone why they're called fightin' cocks.

When it's time for a cock fight to begin, the referee will ask the handlers for the two roosters to come to the center of the pit. Each rooster has to have a handler to keep them under control until the fight begins, as their natural instinct is to fight just as soon as they see or sense another rooster. The handlers will then walk to the center of the pit holdin' their particular fightin' cock. They always hold their cock's legs with one hand so that they don't flail out and hook them with a gaff. As sharp as those gaffs are, they could do major damage to a man's arm, and a couple of the handlers around here have had that happen to them in the past. If you've ever seen a man's arm who's been toed by a gaff, you'll know exactly what I'm talkin' about.

When the two handlers get to the center of the pit, the referee steps in between them and tells 'em to let the roosters "ruff each other up a tad." The handlers then inch slowly towards each other in order to get the two roosters' heads close together. When they get close enough, the two roosters start pecking at each other, which does nothing to improve their dispositions. A half minute or so of this pisses both of 'em off, which means that they're ready to get in the pit and whip each other's feathered asses!

The ref watches all this very closely, and when the time is right, he'll holler, "Pit 'em!" With that, the two handlers will step back a couple of steps and turn their roosters loose. What happens next is about as subtle as a truck full of hogs running into a truck filled with barbed wire—the two fightin' cocks just lay into each other, and the feathers, beaks, gaffs and all are flyin'! And flyin' like scalded dogs! Roosters sort of fight like boxers, they'll tear into one another, step back, regroup, circle a bit, and then tear into each other again. As sharp and as bad as those gaffs are, most times the only major damage one rooster will do to another is hit their opponent in either the eye or heart. That will obviously put a stop to a match, and understand that a match will not stop until one cock is dead or totally incapable of defending itself. A cockfight typically lasts a fairly good while. I've seen a few go as long as forty-five minutes to an hour.

I guess you could say cock fighting is survival of the fittest in its purest sense, and it also happens to be illegal in Georgia. Nonetheless, Uncle Dog, Ed Jr., Coogler, Ed Sr., and many of the other men who live in these parts raise and fight roosters, just as their daddies did before them, and as their granddaddies did before them. Hell, it's so popular around here that Uncle Dog built a small arena way back in the woods where he holds and sponsors these fights. I kid ya'll not—you drive down Highway 87, turn into his place, go down a side road way into the woods, make a couple of turns, and you're there. When you get out of your car you'll see a nice metal-framed building that'll remind you of a small arena. Once you go up to the ticket window to pay your admission fee, you go on in. In the center of the arena is the pit area, a circle of red dirt that's about five feet wide framed by a concrete "fence" that's maybe a foot or so high. Surrounding the pit are sections of what I'd call "stadium seating"—just one-piece sections of seats (similar to what you'd see at a softball field) that surround the pit. In total there are four sections of seats that surround the pit, and they'll seat maybe seventy-five to eighty people. And that's plenty, even though I have seen as many as one hundred plus people attend one of these chicken fights. I'm not kiddin' around when I tell ya'll they are popular.

One thing you'll notice at cock fights is a whole lot of milling around. The reason? Well, at a normal chicken fight probably three out of four people attending are men, and the three big activities that go on at any chicken fight are watching the fights, betting on the fights, and then slipping outside at intervals to enjoy adult oriented refreshments. That's one of the oddest things about a cockfight—inside, while the fights are goin' on, money is bet like a bat out of hell, guys are cussin' like a cat who's just had his ass doused with turpentine. But, if a guy wants to slug down a beer he has to go outside to do it. Chicken fight etiquette, I suppose.

I know I've talked a lot about men and cockfights, so let me say something here about the women that attend. There typically aren't that many, but women at a cockfight pretty much live on pure adrenaline. You can tell it by how they dress. They'll wear the tightest jeans imaginable, and their tits will always be hanging out of their cotton or flannel-type shirts, even when the weather is cold. They stare at the chicken fights, stare even harder at the men, and I honestly think that the combination of bettin', cussin', and violence turns 'em on to no end. I've noticed more than one woman just about beggin' her man to take her home, and I don't think she wants to just sip hot cocoa together once they get there. Chicken fights bring out the tulip honin' gene in women something fierce, and I can only hope one day to reap the benefits of it myself. I just have a feeling that there's no better poontang on this planet than what these chicken fight women dole out.

Man, I'd get better my mind out of vulva central and get back to the business at hand, and that's letting ya'll know a little something about how these chicken fights work. About the only thing left that I can tell ya'll that I haven't talked about already is that we do have a refreshment stand in the arena, so no one goes hungry or anything. I've gotta admit that it's sort of interesting to watch someone up in the stands chomping on popcorn while two fightin' cocks are in the pit fightin' it out to the death. I guess each to his or her own, you know.

Now ya'll know the truth behind one of our biggest holiday events, the Juliette Christmas Cock Fight. One of the main reasons it's held right before Christmas is that it gives the men around here a chance to take home a big pot of money right before the holiday. You see, at a typical cock fight you'll have one or two guys win several hundred dollars each by the time the evening is over, on account of all the bets that are made. Let's face it, a lot of the men attending the fights tonight are poor as Job's turkey, so this cockfight will give them a chance to walk out of here with hundreds of dollars. More than one family around these parts has had a happier than expected Christmas because of cock fight winnings, and I'm sure lots of men will be at tonight's for that very reason. Let's face it—who wouldn't want to go? It's an evening of violence, drinking, betting, and getting to look at the chests of some women that'll make you howl at the moon. I can't say much more about that because this is supposed to be a Christmas story, and it's also making my britches tent up so much that they're reminding me of an Arabian village.

Ed Jr. is gonna take a stable of six roosters in tonight, and he plans on leaving around six-thirty. Looks like Brother and I both are gonna go with him. The fights officially start at eight, and if this one goes like most of 'em, it'll be around one or two in the morning before the last fight ends, the last beer is drunk, and the last chicken fight mama is taken home for some groin-to-groin combat. Ed Jr. always asks my mom several times beforehand if she'd like to go, and she always replies that she would much rather smooch a rattlesnake. I don't even know why he asks her so much, but I guess that's just their pre-fight ritual, so I go with it. It's one of those things that seems to work, even though it makes about as much sense as a priest advising people about sex. But hey, if it works for them, it works for them, so why worry about it?

I kill almost the whole afternoon bullshitting Jenny about why I can't take her out tonight. I don't want to deliberately lie to her, but I don't think it will sit too well with her if she knows that I'm going to spend the whole evening watchin' fightin' cocks live up to their names. I basically tell her that I'm not feelin' good and am really tired, which are both somewhat true—I don't feel good about lyin' to her, and bein' out as late as I'm going to be will surely make me tired, so that part will be true in the next nine to ten hours. Like I said, I don't like lying to her, but I do like to have a little fun sometimes, and I don't think Jenny looks at fun in quite the same way I do. So I'll live with the lie.

Time passes pretty quickly between bullshitting the woman you love and catching bits and pieces of four straight episodes of *Leave It to Beaver*. There's some kind of *Beaver* marathon on one of our local TV stations this afternoon, so I catch bits and pieces of four solid episodes in the midst of all that talkin' with Jenny. I still like watching *Beaver*, as the Eddie Haskell character alone makes it worth it. But you also have to laugh out loud at any show whose main character is named "Beaver." I'm amazed that as straight-laced as these TV networks are that they'd allow a character to even be named that, but they sure did on this particular show. You'd think that Beaver would've inspired other TV characters with names like "Muff Diver", "Hard Dick" and "Woolly Bush" but such is not the case, I'm afraid. It's hard for me not to laugh out loud when June gets on to Ward for being "too hard on the Beaver," but at least I haven't heard her say that when my mom is in the room. That would result in an ass whuppin' and a half for me. Hell, she'd kill me for havin' thoughts like that bouncin' around in my head.

It's startin' to get dark, which means it's gettin' pretty close to time to leave, and I can tell ya'll that I'm mega bundling up tonight as it's going to be colder than all the witches' tits in Georgia put together. I'm actually taking gloves and a jacket with a hood, and I'm definitely gonna wear the thickest pair of jeans that I own. I'm putting on so much shit that I'm thinking I'll make crunching sounds every time I take a step. Better to be sounding like dead leaves being stepped on than for my fingers, toes, or dick to become pink popsicles, that's for sure.

Ed Jr. is already backing the car out of the garage to load it. He always takes our old Ford Falcon whenever he's hauling chickens 'cause the damn thing has a trunk in it that's big enough to live in. It's gotta be three feet deep and a good five feet across, and I'm probably understating both. It would have to be that big for us to haul six roosters over to Dog's secret arena in it, and that's exactly what we're about to do. Ed Jr. has these chicken-toting boxes that he loads each rooster into, and it's sort of fun watching him pluck them out of their coups. A coup is typically just some fencing wire rolled around in a circle with sheet metal top. A little piece of the wire on the side of the coup is cut open with wire snips, and the little flap that results serves as a small door. To get a rooster out of the coup, Ed Jr. opens the door, reaches in, and sometimes he gets lucky and grabs the rooster on his first try. It's pretty important that he does that, cause if he doesn't, the rooster raises holy hell inside that small coup, flapping its wings, crowing and clucking like hell, and sometimes they even shit all over it. If Ed Jr. misses on his first grab, then he has to physically get in the coup with the rooster and let his body mass sort of cut its escape options. The bad thing about doing that is that you're still faced with picking up a frightened, hysterical rooster, and they can do some pretty healthy damage to you with just their regular spurs.

Tonight Ed Jr. is pretty lucky loading his roosters into their boxes, he gets five out of six on his first tries into the coups, and only has to get into a coup with one. The one that he does have to get in there with is worth watching, though, as the rooster involved keeps avoiding Ed Jr.'s grabs over and over and over again. It even flies up into his chest when he has it cornered in the pen. When he finally does grab the enraged rooster, it shits all over the left sleeve of his shirt, which means that he has to go back into the house and change before he can ride over to Uncle Dog's. It's pretty damn hilarious. Ed Jr. is muttering about "what a fucking ingrate" the rooster is, how he feeds him and all, and the thanks he receives for doing that is literally a bunch of shit! The sight of him walking into the house with his shirt off and his left arm stuck out is enough to make Brother and I laugh 'til we hurt ourselves. The old man doesn't stay in the house long, though. He is in and out in a snap, and the clock now shows six-ten, which means that we have to go. We all get in the car, Ed Jr. cranks her up, and we are on our way. I swear that I can still smell a little chicken shit aroma coming off our dad, but it's probably best not to mention that to him.

Ed Jr. slips my brother and me five bucks each on the drive over to Uncle Dog's, which will more than cover us from a snack standpoint over the course of the evening. He also tells me that I'm getting old enough to be a target for some of those chicken fight women now, and that if I go off with one of them, I'm on my own, including explaining what I might do with her to Mama. I honestly can't say that I don't want to go off with a chicken fight woman, but I'll bet that I'd end up with her all night if I did, and I can't even imagine trying to explain it to Mama the next day. I guess I'm in one of those situations where I sort of don't want something to happen, but then again, if it does happen I'll be happy as hell for one night, and then live in Hell itself for a good while after. If the rest of my life is filled with choices like these, I probably ought to consider becoming a monk and just spend my time getting fat and saying long prayers. Well, no need to worry about that, as there's about as much chance of a Williams becoming a monk as there is of Ed Sr. dabbin' perfume behind his ears—it just ain't ever gonna happen.

We soon pull off Highway 87 and begin the less-than-easy-to-drive path back to Uncle Dog's chicken fighting arena. Since it's so deep down in the woods, the only way to it is on this old twisting dirt road. There are several deep holes scattered throughout, and a couple are so deep that your evening's drive will come to a halt if you happen to find one of them. On top of that, there are some marshy areas scattered around that are almost as hazardous as these mini Grand Canyons. We do have one thing going for us, though, and that's Ed Jr.'s familiarity with this road—he knows it like the back of his hand, so I have all the confidence in the world that we'll easily make it through. If I didn't, it would be pretty damn nerve racking when you combine all the potential hazards with those cluckin' chickens back in our trunk. Thankfully, Ed Jr. is working his back roads magic yet again, weaving us through holes and red mud pits that would tingle the balls of even the heartiest explorer.

We pull up to the chicken fighting arena and there are cars all over the place, so I can already tell that we're gonna have a packed house here tonight. There's some nice cars, some piece of shit ones, and there are even a couple of police cars parked out here. I kid ya'll not—Uncle Dog is so well liked, and these fights are so popular that even a few cops attend them. The best thing about having them here is our cops would know in advance if some of the other cops "not in the know" happened to start sniffing out our gaming facility. Hell, even if they caught us red-handed, my money says that Uncle Dog would offer them all some beer and a chance to talk trash with some of these chicken fight women, and the result would be that those cops would be immediately converted over to the cause. Let's face it, what man, cop or not, can resist gambling, beer, and chicken fight women? Hell, I wouldn't even put my money on the Pope if he was given a shot at those pieces of adult candy, and that fact's as solid as a British pencil.

Fortunately, since Ed Jr. is Uncle Dog's brother and a regular chicken fight contestant, we're allowed to park over in a special place that's right next to the main parking area. This place will lead you out onto another dirt road, which will get you out of this bottom much, much quicker. Uncle Dog likes keeping this road a secret because if we really do get raided someday we don't want to be in the middle of some hundred-odd cars all trying to get out on the same dirt road.

With that in mind, we quickly pull over, park, and get out of our car. As soon as we do that I notice it's colder than a well digger's ass already, just one of those deep-down-to-the-bone colds that seem to seep through your skin and make every molecule inside you shiver. Thankfully, I do have some gloves in my pocket, which I desperately don't want to put on as I really think I look like a pussy when I wear 'em, but at least I've got 'em just in case. I'm also wearing two pairs of socks, which is not such a bad idea when you consider that a couple of years ago Jamey Griffin got drunker than hell, took off his shoes, went barefoot, and then ended up with frostbite so bad that the doc almost had to take off his toes. Jamey claimed later on that the reason he got frostbite was that he banged a chicken fight woman out in the back seat of his car, and doing that caused all of his blood to go from his feet to his dick, which made him more susceptible to frostbite. That makes perfect sense to me, and the entire thought makes me doubly glad that

I have my feet, hands, and my dick all warmly covered up tonight.

Brother and I go around to the back of our car to take our roosters out. All six seem to be doing okay, they're clucking and crowing like a bunch of damned poultry hyenas, which is what you want them to be doing. Ed Jr. cusses one of them, as he shit half a brick in the box from just the house to here, but otherwise nothing much of note occurs. The three of us then proceed to take one chicken box in each of our hands and walk them all over to the staging area for the fights, a little building close to the arena that's really just a small barn. It's the perfect place for staging these fights, as there's plenty of space for any man who's entering roosters to get his lined up and squared away. There's also plenty of hay on the ground, which is good for the heavier drinkers to lie down on later on, and it's also good for something else, which I discovered further on into the evening.

Ed Jr., Brother and I find one of the old horse stalls and set up shop there. My dad then organizes his roosters in the order he wants to fight them tonight. In chicken fighting, you get so many points for each fight, based on the quality of the roosters. The worst roosters are called "dunghills." These are roosters who've never fought or haven't shown themselves to be very aggressive when they're out with the other chickens. You can tell a lot about the quality of a good fighting cock when they're just out in the yard on a day-to-day basis. The best ones can't even be out with the others as they'll start up a scrap on their own. And there's nothing worse than a natural chicken fight. A staged fight like tonight, as strange as it sounds, is much more humane than just letting them fight it out in the backyard. In a staged fight, the gaffs bring an end to it much sooner than out in one's backyard, and with much less blood and guts. And the worst ones? The worst ones won't even get in there and hustle for some feed when it's thrown to them. They'll just peck around at the edges, too damned timid to get in there and hustle it out with the other chickens. Ole Coogler actually ran a rooster out of his yard one time because it wouldn't get in there and scrap for some food. As Ed Jr. says, "It's a piss poor man that won't try to feed himself, and it's even worse when a game rooster does the same thing."

Once you decide on the order of the roosters you're entering for the fight, you write them all down on a card and take it over to the referee. The referee will take all the cards from everyone who's entering roosters and then draw up the match-ups. It's extremely important that the ref be someone who's impartial and who'll match up the roosters just as evenly as he possibly can. A bad referee can cause a lot of bad will among people, and that's the best case scenario. The worst case is that an ass whippin' or two gets doled out after some bad refereein', and those ass whippins' aren't just between the chicken fighters. The referee himself can lose a few teeth if they mess up too bad.

Looks like that won't be a problem for us tonight as Mike McDowell, one of the fairest guys around here, is handlin' the refereein' duties. Ed Jr. has known Mike for a long time, and get this, Mike is an attorney. I shit you not. Our ref tonight is an attorney! Seems to be doin' real well at it, too. He has more cases to work than he can handle, and the word is that he might try to run for one of these area-type judges' positions one day. And ya'll can laugh for what I'm about to say, but Mike is pretty shrewd. He picks up new friends and potential campaign supporters every time he calls one of these chicken fights. Let's face it, a lot of money is on the line at these things, and a lot of personal pride is on the line as well. If you fight roosters and yours gets his ass whupped, well, it's just like gettin' your own ass whupped. That's how all true chicken fighters regard it, so it's really important to them that the ref handles the fights well and leaves nothing open for interpretation—he has to call it right down the middle. If he does, the winners leave happy and the losers reluctantly accept their defeats. If he doesn't, more than one scrap can break out as at least a couple of guys will have a true championship case of the red ass, and be itchin' to do something about it. The worst case is that several scraps break out, and the cops are forced to deal with both the scraps and the chicken fightin'. If that ever happens, these cock fights will come to a screechin' halt for good.

Ed Jr. takes his card over to Mr. McDowell, and me and Brother decide to go in the arena and case things out. It's already bustling all around the entrance, and it takes almost fifteen minutes to get up to the front of the ticket line. My Aunt Clara is taking up the money, and she smiles at Brother and me when she sees us and waves us on in. Aunt Clara is a great lady, as down to earth as it gets, and a true woman. She has to be to live with my Uncle Dog on a day-to-day basis. Don't get me wrong, I love Uncle Dog to death, but he's a man that never sees a party he doesn't want to join, never sees a drink of liquor that he doesn't want to have, and never sees a pretty woman that he doesn't want to slip the ole one-eyed heat-seeking trouser snake to. Aunt Clara has to be one helluva woman to wrestle with all that, and she does a damn good job of it. And then some.

When we get inside, there's people all over the place. It's like an anthill that's been stirred up with a stick! I guess a lot of people want a shot at that early Christmas money, and bets are already startin' to be made, even before they know whose rooster is fightin' whose. People are even bettin' on the owners. I hear a bet made for twenty dollars that Coogler will do better overall than Ed Jr., and then another one for ten bucks that Jim Starr's roosters will outfight everyone else's. Randy Lilliott is already two sheets to the wind, and he wants to bet on how many times Mr. Jumbo Summers, the pool hall owner in Forsyth, will fart out loud during the fights. Mr. Summers is a great guy, but he blasts out those frapping-type farts, the ones that almost seem to ripple out of the person like waves in the ocean.

Funny thing is, three other guys want a piece of the Summers fart bet, so a pool gets started—throw two bucks in the hat, and guess how many times Mr. Summers will play notes on his ass tuba this evening. There are several guys lining up to put their money in, and word gets around to Mr.

Summers, who's sitting way across on the other side of the arena. When someone whispers the details of this tender bet to him, Mr. Summers smiles, hikes up his leg, and blasts out his first methane burger of the night, a nice, full, pungent blast. Most of the guys around him laugh, and Brad Hawk prays out loud that he doesn't fart anymore, as his number in the fart pool is "one," which means a twenty to thirty dollar payoff for him based on the number of guys who've entered the over/under Summers fart pool.

Brother and I continue ambling around the arena and two chicken fight women come walkin' towards us. They're two women I've never seen before, and it doesn't look like they're with anyone, as normally women who attend chicken fights have their husbands or boyfriends with them. This is even more emphasized by the fact that one of them is smoking a small cigar and the other one isn't wearing a bra, not that it bothers me any. The braless one has great boobs; they seem to be heavy and are jiggling up under her top like two full plates of Jell-O. I'm really enjoying watchin' the ripples, the only problem being that I stay too focused on her chest as she gets closer and closer to me. I don't realize just how close until I hear the woman attached to that chest say, "Boy, if you look at my titties any harder than you are, I may have to pull one out and nurse you right here in front of God and everybody!"

Well, she says that really loud, and the only thing louder are the laughs from everybody else right after she says it. I'll bet that a good hundred or so people are all cackling over my hormone-induced trance. It's embarrassing and then some—shit, even Brother is laughing right along with them. My face gets all red and flushed, I feel like I need to pee, and I just can't find any words to respond with. Well, that just encourages this old gal, so she grabs me and kisses me, figurin' that I will fold up like a house of cards. Well, she makes a little mistake when she does that. I may be young, and she may have just embarrassed the hell out of me, but I'm a Williams, and a Williams that's being kissed hard by a big-tittied chicken fight woman. I kiss her right back, givin' her the ole lizard tongue and puttin' everything I have into it. I can just feel the surprise in her, the whole arena rocks out with laughter over this turn of events, and now this ole chicken fight gal is the one who really doesn't know what to do. When our smooch ends, I just look at her, smile, and walk away. And walk away feeling pretty damned good about myself, not that I'm braggin', mind you.

Brother tells me that we ought to sit down before every seat has an ass in it, and he's right—this place is filling up faster than a lawnmower engine. When it's cold like this it's a lot better to be sittin' in the stands with people all around you than to be standing out in these cold drafts and breezes. It's especially good if you happen to get an old fat gal sittin' close to you, as the heat coming off her can keep you pretty damned comfortable for the rest of the evening. It may or may not be a coincidence, but do ya'll ever notice how seldom you see any older single fat women? Let's face it, they keep you warm at night, and they can obviously cook, so they get taken off the market fast. Hey, I'm young, but I do pick up on things from time to time, so I'm already feelin' a tad smarter as I take my seat here and wait for the evening's festivities to commence. We've got awhile to go, maybe thirty or so minutes, but our only other choice is walkin' around and bein' so cold that our toes go numb, so on our asses sittin' here we will be.

Brother lucks out, as he most times does, and is sittin' next to Jerry Hairell, a guy from Forsyth that we both know who's attending these fights for the first time. Jerry loves sports. He can talk about those sorry assed Braves and Falcons all day long, and he and Brother immediately get to talkin' about all kinds of sports shit. And, pray tell, who do I have sittin' next to me? Why, it's Fuzz-Mouth Isbell, who may be one of the all-time stupidest shits in the history of the world. Fuzz-Mouth gets his name because the color of his teeth alternates between yellow and green, and his teeth are just a starting point. Fuzz-Mouth has to be, without question, one of the stupidest people alive. He makes Omar Stafford look like a Ph.D., and that's saying a whole lot right there.

Just to give ya'll an idea of how stupid he is, one time

he decided to trim the hedges in front of his house by cranking up his lawn mower and then holding it over the hedges. I kid ya'll not, he cranked the damn thing up and tried to hold it over his hedges. For being that mentally vacant, he lost three of the fingers on his right hand. Fuzz-Mouth doesn't let that stop him, either. On another occasion he let some guys convince him that the best way to get honey out of a bee hive was to draw all of the bees out of it. And just how do you do that? Well, they told Fuzz-Mouth that the best way was to rub honey all over yourself and then go stand in front of a hive. Fuzz-Mouth did exactly that, going over to Jim Banks' house one afternoon because Jim has a few bee hives in his back yard. Fuzzie went at a time when he knew Jim wouldn't be home, and when he got there he stripped down to his boxers and then rubbed honey all over his arms and legs. The only problem with his plan was that Jim's wife happened to be home, and she witnessed this tender scene as it unfolded in her back yard. She then called the police, which turned out to be a good thing as they got there just in time to see about a million bees swarming all over ole Fuzz Mouth. It took the cops a good twenty minutes just to hose them all off him, and in the process he received twenty-five to thirty stings. Fortunately, Fuzz Mouth isn't allergic to bee stings, and, according to the cops, the swelling from the stings really didn't do much to hurt his looks. Bottom line, ole Fuzz Mouth is close to being a three-bag haint, the only thing he has going for him is that he has one helluva head full of blonde hair. He's so blonde that it would put Nature Boy Buddy Rogers to shame, and that keeps him from being a haint up there in the league with Charlie Pound. Anyway, when you're a haint like he is, swelling from bee stings or anything else isn't really gonna make much of a difference.

However bad a haint he is, I'm sitting right next to him, and Fuzzie proceeds to elbow me in the ribs and say, *"HEY, ED MAN!"* Fuzz Mouth says nothing softly, everything he says is louder than a smoky-tailed dog, and he's being loud right in my ear at point-blank range. Another problem I've got is the fact that the breath whizzing through his moss-covered teeth smells like the ass end of a dead farm mule. I can already see that there's no way in hell that I'm going to survive twenty minutes of this, so my mind goes into a self defense mode, which means that my eyes are going all around the room trying to find something or somebody who will get me out of this predicament. Finally, over to our right are the two women that I just had all that fun with, and the big tittied one spies me lookin' at her. To her credit, she smiles back, laughs, and winks. I then grab ole Fuzz-Mouth by the shoulder, point over to where my mammary queen is sittin', and start priming him that she's actually lookin' at him. Ole Fuzz Mouth looks over at her, and sure enough, she is still smiling and laughing, and he takes this to mean that she might be a tad sweet on him.

Ya'll need to understand something about somebody like Fuzz-Mouth. He's never had any attention from a woman in his life, and just the chance of it will make his hormones, dick, throat, and any of his other body parts buzz with excitement. I decide that the best thing to do is to really build him up, and try to make him believe that this pretty, big bosomed gal is all hot and bothered over him. So, each time she laughs I whisper to the Fuzzer that she's looking at him and obviously likes what she sees. The poor bastard gets so worked up that he's not even talkin' anymore, he just nods right along with anything I tell him. I figure it's now time to go for broke, so I lean over and tell the Fuzzer that it's apparent that this gal wants to get to know him better, and he needs to get up and go talk to her. Fuzzie asks me if I'm really sure about this, and I tell him that I've never been surer of anything in my life. He smiles, says a loud, *"THANK YOU, BUDDY,"* and then gets up out of his seat and starts making his way over to the swollen-chested gal. I breathe a super huge sigh of relief 'cause I know that his seat will be taken in ten seconds, which it is, and then I realize that this place is so full of people that we can barely move. It's so bad that the referee orders some of the people to stand outside of the arena as we have a potential safety hazard mounting here in the building. One of the cops who's here seconds the motion, and about forty or fifty people are told to go stand outside the building. Whoever goes is promised that someone will come out every few minutes and tell them how the fights are going, and they're also promised that this same person will place bets for them. This makes leaving the arena a bit easier to take, and about forty or so people get up and walk outside. Oh, it also may have helped that Uncle Dog promised half priced beer to anyone who "goes out for the good of all."

Once the building is thinned down, the ref announces that the fights are going to begin. The handlers come out with the first two roosters, and it's time to rock and roll. Bets are being made all over the place, and lo and behold, who do I see over in the far corner of the arena but Ed Sr. My granddad is making so many bets that he's writing 'em all down on a piece of paper. This is a tad unusual, 'cause Ed Sr. is real sporadic about attending these chicken fights—he loves the fights but he hates being up late, and with all the entries in tonight's fights, this thing could go on until two or three o'clock in the morning. Brother and I will be here however long it goes, as Ed Jr. will be in the midst of all of it, but I doubt the old man will stay for more than an hour or two. Based on the number of bets he's placing, it's obvious he's going to make his hour or two count. God, he's writing them down like a possessed man…

Mr. McDowell lets the two roosters peck themselves into a frenzy, and then he yells to the handlers, "Step back!" This tells the handlers that they are about to pit 'em, and sure enough, that's exactly what Mr. McDowell says next. And brother, when he does, these two roosters just lock into each other. All you can see are feathers, legs, and gaffs flailing the air and each other, and that's me being nice about it. There's nothing subtle about two fightin' cocks, they're there to whip their opponent's ass and do it as quickly as possible. Mr. McDowell, the ref, really has no control over these two chickens. One of them either is going to kill the other or they're both going to collapse from exhaustion and injuries. While they're in there fighting, people are entranced by the spectacle, and everything else, the concession sales, bets, etc. all grind to a temporary halt. The two combatants, of course, are oblivious to all this, as they are engaged in a dance that only one of them will remember the outcome of.

As the feathers fly, one rooster jumps up in the air, flails out with his feet, and sinks his gaff well into the neck of his opponent. He finds the right spot, and his opponent slumps into the dirt, vanquished by a single, well-placed blow. The winner is then announced to the crowd by the ref, and you can tell that the bets on this fight were pretty even, as about half the crowd is cheering and the other half is calling the dead rooster's relatives a string of cuss words that I wouldn't even call an Italian communist. It's pretty bad, but I do notice over in the corner that Ed Sr. is smiling. He has good reason to do so, as a string of fellows are making their way over towards him with their money out. I really can't see the bills from where I'm sitting, but he has to have made at least fifty to seventy-five dollars off of this one bet alone. One thing I'll give to the old man is that he knows how to make money. His store is profitable, plus he owns a lot of land that he bought during depression times when you could get land for twenty-five to fifty cents an acre. Ed Sr. bought up a bunch of land at those prices, and it's worth a good bit more now. So, if I think about all that, I guess it really shouldn't surprise me that he's just won a big bet. Him and money just seem to have an understanding, I suppose.

In the midst of watching all the hoopla and the movement of money between the men, I barely notice that the next two fightin' cocks have been brought out. Everyone else sure has noticed, 'cause the betting for this fight is even more frenzied than it was for the first one. Big Lick John Mullins is over in one corner betting his damn overalls on this fight—I'm serious, he's literally betting his damn overalls! As near as I can make out, Big Lick shot his proverbial wad by betting too much on the first fight and all he has to his name that's worth anything now is the brand new pair of Sears Roebuck overalls that he's wearing. What makes this all the worse is that he has a taker for his bet. Ned Willis is putting up ten bucks against his overalls. That brings a lot of laughter from everyone, but get this—Johnny Whitehead, a local farmer and a man who could drink up the Atlantic Ocean if it was made out of beer, has offered to put up an extra five dollars on the bet, with the stipulation that if Big Lick loses, he has to hand those overalls over to Ned Willis as soon as the fight is over. Big Lick doesn't want to take him up on it, but the crowd starts hollerin' and yellin', and a couple of the men make comments that Big Lick doesn't want to drop his drawers because then his nickname will have to be changed from "Big Lick" to "Little Dick." With that being said, all Big Lick can do is take the bet and hope like hell that his rooster has a lot of piss and vinegar inside him tonight.

One thing I notice as the referee brings the handlers to the center of the pit for this fight is that everyone runs over to the concession stand right after all the bets are made. For awhile I couldn't understand this, but it makes more sense to me now. There's a lot of pressure on these men tonight—I know it's a cock fight and it's all supposed to be fun, but a bunch of these men really are hoping to make some money so that their Christmas is a little brighter. A losing night means that a family might end up with just a few stockings loaded with walnuts and raisins to give their children on Christmas morning, and that sucks just about any way you happen to look at it. Ed Sr. has sworn to me over the years that he and my Uncle Frank actually whipped Santa's ass on Christmas Eve one year when he was a boy, due to Santa only bringing them some walnuts and raisins the year before. I don't know if I believe him or not, but any way you cut it, a Christmas morning with nothing but walnuts and raisins in it is just about like buying your sister a negligee. Why bother? Anyway, I think there's so much pressure on these guys to win their bets that they have to go get some refreshments right after they place them, maybe some Pabst Blue Ribbon is just the thing to sooth the soul before these fighting cocks get down to business.

The big news in this fight is that one rooster in it belongs to Ed Jr., and the other belongs to Uncle Dog, which means that it's pretty hard to know just who to root for. I usually always want my dad to win, but Uncle Dog is a very cool guy, so it's hard for me to pull against him. To tell ya'll the truth, I actually sort of hope my dad loses this one, as this rooster he's entered is a real bastard, and that's me putting it mildly. He crows all the damn time, day or night, and I've never seen a rooster that shits as much as this one. On a good day he'll leave turds all over the backyard, which makes things really sweet in the summertime when you'd like to go barefooted outside. This rooster needs to lose in the worst way, and then he can go crap all over rooster heaven for the rest of eternity. Of course, Ed Jr. will never know my true feelings on this, but down deep I'm pulling for Uncle Dog all the way on this one.

Mr. McDowell has the handlers stop the roosters from sparring, so the fight is about to begin. And right when that happens I feel someone slip over and sit next to me. I'm so caught up in the excitement of this fight that I really am not paying attention. But I regain my focus when this very feminine voice whispers in my ear, "Remember me? You and my chest were getting acquainted a little while ago."

I spin around and see that it's the gal with the big knockers that I spoke to earlier. For some reason she's decided to come over and sit next to me. I'm sort of hoping that she likes how I look or something, but then she says, "Boy, I just had to get away from that Fuzz-Mouth rube that showed up a little while ago. He started talkin' to me, and if I told you his breath smelled like shit it would be a compliment. He's a toad, just horrible, and with the mind of a hog who's been sick for a really long time. I was just about to leave, it got so bad over there with him. Then I looked around and saw that the seat next to you had opened up, so I decided that a dose of you was a whole lot better than a dose of the Mossy Creek bandit over there."

Well, it's not exactly a boost to my pride, but I admire her honesty and laugh out loud. She laughs right along with me, and then our attention quickly turns to the matter at hand, that being the scrap between Ed Jr.'s and Uncle Dog's roosters.

I can tell that Big Lick must've bet on Ed Jr.'s, 'cause every time that bird flaps a wing he starts rooting like hell for him. As for me, I'm silently rooting for Uncle Dog's rooster, and then something happens that causes me to pull for him even more. And that something is the chicken fight lady, who leans over and whispers to me, "Honey, I love watching these fights, but it's just not as good without a little wager on the outcome. Do you think that we can work us up a little bet on this fight, just something to make it interesting?"

Well, I instantly think of what I'd love to win from her, some tang ala poon, but I don't think she'll put that particular item up on the betting table. I also know that I don't have but a coupla bucks in my pocket, so it's not like I can make a high stakes bet or anything. I figure the best path forward is to be totally honest with her, so I reply, "Ma'am, I only have a couple of bucks on me, but if bettin' something will make you happy, I'm game. What do you wanna do?"

Geez, I'm trying to sound all cool and all, but I say all these words right into her blouse, and she knows it, too. Funny thing, though—instead of getting all pissed about it, she smiles, looks right at me, and says, "I know the perfect bet for you and me."

Needless to say, I'm interested in what that might be, so I ask the obvious, "And what would that be, ma'am?"

"Honey, first off, my name is Sylvia, not ma'am. Call me Sylvia, please. Second, I think you ought to put up those two dollars against some scenery."

"Some scenery? I don't get it."

Sylvia then makes my night when she says, "Honey, if I lose this bet, we'll walk outside someplace private, and I'll let you take a nice, long look at what I'm keeping inside this blouse."

She's tellin' me she's gonna let me see her knockers if I win! Holy shit! Believe me, I try to act all cool about it, but I accept her bet faster than Ex-Lax cycles through a goose. In fact, I accept so quickly that she laughs out loud, and then she asks, "Baby, would you go get me a beer? I'm already enjoyin' these fights a whole lot more than I was."

Well, if ya'll don't think I scramble my ass on down to the concession stand to get her a beer, ya'll are crazy. My only problem is that my Aunt Clara won't sell me one because I'm still a tad under-aged. Then, when I try to explain to her that it isn't for me, but for a friend, she asks to see just who my new "friend" is. And when I point her out, she shakes her head and says, "You Williams men have one thing in common—a pretty woman can turn your heads, but a pretty woman with big boobs can turn your heads, your hearts, your wallets, and your privates. Here, take this, run on back and make your 'friend' happy. And Edward?"

"Yes ma'am?"

"Be careful after you take that beer back."

Well, I walk back and take that beer up to my seat, and once back in it, I hand it over to Sylvia. She takes a sip, smiles real big, then sort of looks up and down at me and says, "Honey, I'm starting to like you more and more and more. You seem to know what I like."

To that, I suavely reply, "That's great!"

We don't have any more time to talk, as Ed Jr.'s and Uncle Dog's roosters are going at it like there's no tomorrow. The action is so fast and furious that the two roosters remind me of real life versions of Tasmanian Devils, just asses and feathers with all the whirring and movement that goes along with it. The people in the stands seem to be pretty evenly divided on this fight, so it's obvious that the betting line on it is basically a toss-up. I look over at Big Lick, and he is focused on it like a rabbit's focused on his pecker, and Ed Jr. and Uncle Dog are riveted to it like it's the bottom of the ninth inning of the seventh game of the World Series. I think that's because the Williamses are so competitive, we honest to God can't stand to lose at anything. I remember a couple of years ago we were out at Ed Sr.'s and Miss Lily's one Christmas, and Uncle Bob showed everyone a new set of golf clubs that his girlfriend had given him. Calhoun (my uncle Jerry) remarked that with no practice at all he could hit a golf ball further than anyone there.

Ed Jr. responded that he was full of shit, and even my Uncle Jew said that he wanted a piece of that action. It led to them all going out into the front yard and trying out those new clubs. If I remember right, Uncle Dog hit his the farthest and Uncle Calhoun shanked his off into the woods, which led all the others to tell him he was light in the loafers and worse. It was pure vintage Williams, and a situation that I've seen repeated many times since. And now another chapter is taking place right here in this very pit, and quite a violent chapter indeed.

Ed Jr.'s rooster angles over to one side of the pit and leans against the concrete wall, appearing to be just about out of it. Uncle Dog's cautiously walks over to deliver the grand finale and discovers that it's just a bit too soon. Ed Jr.'s rooster snaps to attention and flies all over Uncle Dog's. I don't know if Ed Jr.'s rooster is smart enough to play possum, or if its impending death causes it to give it everything it has but, whatever the reason, Ed Jr.'s rooster is now kicking Uncle Dog's rooster's ass, and I don't like that one bit. Not with me having a chance to look at whatever Sylvia here is willing to show me up under her blouse. I figure that I'll just silently pull like hell for Uncle Dog, so as not to give anything away, but I can't even begin to tell ya'll how badly I want his cock to win. Geez, that sounds pretty perverted given the situation, but that's the bottom line. Ya'll know what I mean.

Sylvia must sense my enthusiasm, 'cause she snuggles up close to me and purses her shoulders so that I can get a nice little peak right down her blouse. God, she has some of those never-ending bazookas, nice full boobs whose cleavage just never seems to end. I also notice that she's wearing the skimpiest little bra you could ever imagine, just lace cups that are overflowing with some prime Grade A titty. Man, if ya'll thought that I wanted to see her personal geography before, just multiply that by sixty or seventy now. My whole body feels like a lit firecracker, and I think there's only one known way to get that feeling out of my system…

'Bout the time I finish with that thought, Ed Jr.'s rooster hangs a gaff right through the middle of Uncle Dog's rooster's chest, which means that he scores a direct hit to the heart. Uncle Dog's rooster drops quicker than a pre-paid whore, and my heart might as well have been pierced, too—so close to seeing Sylvia's chest, yet all I'm gonna get out of all this is the loss of two one dollar bills. I do the decent thing and pull the money out of my pocket in order to pay Sylvia, but she smiles, hugs me, and says that I have to do more than just pay off the bet. When I ask her what "more" means, she tells me to go buy two beers and meet her out behind the barn. I nod, smile, and then hoof it over to the concession stand where I have to do some mighty tall talkin' to get my Aunt Clara to hand over two beers. After assuring her for about five minutes that I am not going to personally drink one, she relents and lets me have them. She also tells me that Sylvia was eyeing me like a honey bee does a daisy, which causes me to smile a whole bunch of my teeth at her before I can even think about how she'd react. Aunt Clara reacts alright, she rolls her eyes, mutters something about the Williams' men bein' the horniest group of individuals she'd ever seen, and then waves me away so that some of the other customers could get to the front of the line. I am more than happy to oblige her.

I don't want Sylvia to think that I am too excited to get back with her, so I run but don't quite run. Ya'll know what I mean, I walk like I need to take a major crap but never quite break into a jog, so it's like I'm either running in slow motion or walking in fast motion. Whatever the motion, I have to work my way through more people than I've seen all night up to this point—it appears that the night's big fight is going to feature Uncle Dog's primest fighting cock up against Coogler's best, which is a main event match anyway you want to look at it. It's funny, Uncle Dog and Coogler are the best of friends, but in this situation friendship will have to take a back seat. There's a lot of pride on the line in these fights, and a big match-up like this will draw more bets than you'll ever be able to imagine. Well, at least it'll draw bets from those here who can still make them, 'cause I already see a couple of people who've already lost big, and among them is one of the new attendees from the

Sheriff's Department. He started out the evening big talkin,' tryin' to impress everybody with his badge and all, and since then he's gone from talkin' to impress us to placin' some big bets in order to see if that would work. Some of the more experienced betters here smelled him out pretty quickly, so his ass has already been clipped like a new Marine recruit's locks, right down to the bone. Hell, Ed Sr. alone has gotten close to a hundred dollars from him, and apparently he's not the only one skinnin' his ass. Uncle Bob is totin' twenty of his dollars, and I think that Ed Jr. has skinned off fifteen. Hell, if this young cop keeps bettin,' he may finance the entire Williams family Christmas this year. Alas, it doesn't appear that's gonna be possible now, as it looks like this guy is about to call it an evening and go on home. He's tryin' to slip quietly out a side door, but some of the more vocal in the crowd notice and start callin' him a pussy, tellin' him that he's an air britches and worse. You can tell that this guy is madder than two ticks on a one-eared dog, but he still goes ahead and leaves. Well, good riddance I say, he should've kept his smartass mouth shut, and besides, I've talked too much about all this chicken fight stuff, I have much better business to attend to outside!

I finally slip my way through the crowd and find myself out back behind the barn. I'm all keyed up to see Sylvia, and sure enough, she's back there, but there's some big old shit from over in Jones County with her. I think he's one of those Washburn boys, and he's talkin' shit to her like the guy behind the curtain in the *Wizard of Oz*. Since he's a grown man in his late twenties, I know damn well that Sylvia is going to keep all her attention focused on him. I'm disappointed about it and all, and I figure I'll just go back in and give these two beers to somebody else.

A funny thing happens, though. As soon as I start walkin' away, I hear Sylvia say, "Where are you goin', baby? You owe me a beer, darlin'." I turn around to be sure I'm not hearin' things, and I see the Washburn guy walkin' off and her smiling at me like I've got a platinum dick or something. I give her a beer, and then she does the damndest thing…she reaches over, pulls me close, and kisses me, *hard!* No peck on the lips, mind you, she is kissin' me like her tongue is trying to find some hidden gold in my mouth. It makes me feel like I have a nuclear power generator in my chest, and things get even better when the kiss ends and she says, "Baby, let's go walk out to my car."

I nod yes faster than Superman changes clothes, and we walk out towards her car. As it turns out, her car is parked way down at the end of the main parking area, so it takes us a pretty good while to make our way to it. As we walk towards our destination, she slips her hand around my waist and reaches down and squeezes one of the cheeks of my ass. I figure that if she can do that to me that I can do the same, so I do, and her butt feels so good that it's like someone has dipped my hand in gold or something. I don't understand at all why any of this is happenin,' but I don't care. Squeezing a woman's ass, after all, is squeezing a woman's ass. She smiles real brightly at me, I return the same, and after each of us have worked out our hand muscles over and over and over, we find ourselves standing at her car.

Her car, if the truth be told, isn't very much, just an old '68 Chevy Impala, but it's big enough to haul cattle around in. It's a huge-ass car, and, interestingly enough, the back seat has a pillow and a blanket laying on it. We both climb into the front, and as soon as we shut the doors, Sylvia gives me one of those heart and dick thumping-type kisses—ya'll know, the kind that make both organs twitch and skip a beat or two. Before I can even catch my breath, she suggests that we get in the back seat together so that we can "get even better acquainted."

I climb right over the top of the front seat and am in the back one faster than the Flash could've done it. Sylvia laughs, tells me that she likes a man who's eager, and then tells me she's going to give me some further incentive. With that, she whips off her top, and there, in the moonlight, jiggling around before me like two twin pools of pink Jell-O, are two of the nicest sweater bombs that I've ever seen in my life. Granted,

I'm just sixteen, so I haven't seen too many sweater bombs yet, but these are the two all-time best so far, and the best by twenty miles or better. My mouth starts watering, and when she gets in the back seat with me it's all I can do not to beg her to give me some lovin' right then and there. Sylvia can tell that I'm wantin' her really bad, so she kisses me several times, and her smooches cause my pink love sausage to stand up like an interstate exit sign. It's so stiff that it is hurting, so I decide to shift around a little in the seat to relieve some of the pressure. She must sense that I'm feeling discomfort, so she glances down and finds out what's causing the problem. Smiling, she glances over at me and says, "You've all stove up, aren't you baby? I think you're sweet on me, that's what I think. Baby, do you want to tell me what's on your mind? And is there anything I can do to make you feel all better?"

I'm so worked up by this point that there's no hesitation left in me. I am quite willing to tell her just exactly what is on my mind, and what I need from her to make me feel better. And I'm about to tell her, when a person runs right by our car.

No foolin'—a person just runs right by our car, there's absolutely no mistaking it. You can hear their feet hittin' the ground as they run by, and I even catch a glimpse of them as they do. The wild thing is that before we can both look out the window to see who they are, another person, this one a woman, runs by the car as well. Not the usual thing that happens at a chicken fight, for sure. I think the best thing to do is to get out of the car and see what's going on. So I do exactly that, and honest to God, what I'm seeing is a whole slew of people running or walkin' real fast like towards their cars. Very real fast like.

Sylvia sticks her head out the window, looks around, and tells me that I have to get away from her and the car, 'cause she can't afford for anyone to see her carryin' on with a teenaged boy. I tell her that I'd like to call her sometime, but she tells me that our romance has just ended, and punctuates her point by rolling up the window and cranking up her car. Since I can see that things between us are done, I figure that I'd better get back over to the arena and find out just what in the hell is goin' on. And I do just that, runnin' back toward the building through all these people makin' time out towards their cars. The way they're runnin' makes me figure that something terrible must have happened inside. Thoughts hit me like maybe a fire has broken out, or someone has gotten into a fight and has gotten hurt really badly, or maybe something even worse has happened. The more I think about it all, the more worried I become about Ed Jr. and Brother, so I double-time it back in order to check on them and make sure that things are okay.

I run like I'd eaten a Mexican dinner two hours ago, so it doesn't take me very long to get to the arena. Soon as I get there I run right on inside and see that there is no one in there. Well, no one except for Aunt Clara and Misty. They are shuttin' down the concession stand, so I run up to them and ask what in the hell is goin' on. Aunt Clara tells me that someone has called in the cockfight to some people over at the sheriff's department who are not very well disposed towards them. They're on their way over, and if they find bettin' and cockfights goin' on, most of the participants would be goin' to jail, including Ed Jr. That's all I need to know, so I ask Aunt Clara if she knows where my dad is. She tells me that he's out back loadin' up his chickens, and that I need to find him and then we all need to get the hell out of here just as fast as we can. I nod, thank her, and then quickly make the inside of the arena a memory.

I find Ed Jr. out in his stall boxing up his last couple of fighting cocks—when he sees me, he hollers, "Al, I don't know where in the hell you've been, but you and me and Brother need to load up these damn fightin' cocks and get the T-total hell out of here!"

He doesn't have to tell me again. I grab a couple of our chicken-toting boxes and head right out for the car. Brother and Ed Jr. do the exact same thing, and we three double-time it like brand new Army recruits. We cover the distance quickly, load four of the boxes into the trunk, and two get loaded into the back seat. As soon as all that is done, Brother jumps in the back seat, I ride shotgun, and Ed Jr. fires up the old Falcon.

It's actually sort of exciting, you know, sort of like being in one of those big car chase scenes that you see in the movies sometimes. Ed Jr. isn't excited about it one bit, however. He keeps sayin' that if we're caught he'll go to jail, and how it totally pisses him off that some pansy has finked us all out. He then pulls our car out of our secret parking area and onto a little dirt road that we'd normally hang a left on. This time, however, we take a right, a way that I know will take us deeper into the woods. I ask Ed Jr. why we're goin' this way, and he tells me that the cops will be all over Highway 87 like flies on cow shit, and that he isn't goin' to take any chances with that. According to him, the best thing for us to do is to go on further into the woods, wait things out, and then make our way back out onto the highway.

That's exactly what we do. We drive our Falcon a good fifteen miles deeper into the woods, if not further. We're in there so deep that you can see nothing but blackness with just a tiny hint of moonlight, and it's here that Ed Jr. pulls us off the road into a small cleared area with a stream running through it. He cuts off the car and douses the lights, as we sure don't want to call any undue attention to ourselves. We then proceed to get out of the car, eyeball things, and see that we aren't in too bad a place. It's real quiet, has natural running water, and we have the world's biggest restroom in which to take a piss if the need arises. Ed Jr. tells us that if anyone gets really cold he will crank the car back up and cut on the heater so that we can thaw out in it. It's funny, we spend most of our time outside at the chicken fights, but it doesn't seem cold to us because we're all so busy and focused on what is going on. Out here in the darkness, with this little fear wiggling around inside me because of our situation, the cold seems to be more intense. It's like it's settling right into my bones. I hate this kind of cold, it's like you just can't get rid of it no matter what you do, and it makes me wonder why northerners want to be northerners and put up with it all the time. Not to overly knock them, but being up north has to be pure hell. The food sucks, the women are not what you'd call mega attractive, and those Yankee accents that they talk with would strip the hide off a warthog. It just seems to suck as a region of the country to live in, and then some. To live there means that you would just have to accept being colder than hell all the time, and I just couldn't do it. And I won't, either.

I'm wonderin' just what the three of us are gonna do to while away the couple of hours that Ed Jr. says we need to lay low, and I figure that I may as well get the first-hand scoop on just what exactly transpired a few minutes ago. I point-blank ask him about it, and he says that they all thought that the young smartass cop that got his ass skinned on the bets called into the Sheriff's Office and told 'em that he had discovered a cockfight. When he did that, it would've forced a couple of cops to go out to Uncle Dog's and bust things up, since cockfights are illegal and all. Ed Jr. also tells us that not everyone in the Sheriff's Department is crazy about these cockfights, which I'm not aware of, so that would give those officers even more incentive to arrest some of the organizers. And since Ed Jr. is one of the organizers he figures the safest thing for us to do is wait it out until we're sure that all the cops have gone. Brother and I both tell him we don't mind the wait. Actually, other than the cold, this is kinda neat. It's almost like being fugitives on the run. Sometimes I think that I'm going to end up in hot water when I grow up, because I love women too much, I love fun too much, and something like this isn't even bothering me a whole helluva lot.

I can't say the same for Ed Jr. though, he's walking back and forth, cussin', pacin', and then cussin' some more. It's obvious that something's on his mind, and I figure that he's still pissed off at that young cop for finking all of us out. Finally, I guess he gets tired of the quiet, so he starts talkin' about being really pissed off at the fact that a lot of people didn't get a chance to win any real Christmas money this year. On top of that, it turns out that the biggest winner this evening is Ed Sr., who won just a shade over five hundred dollars, and that does not make his son here very happy.

"Let's face it," he says, "the wealthiest man there wins all the money, and that's not fair anyway you look at it. Most of those ole boys really needed that money to even have a chance at a decent Christmas, but they're goin' home with empty pockets. On the other hand, my old man, the most well to do fucker in attendance, walks home with all the money. I don't begrudge anybody there anything, but it just ain't right. He'll just spend the money on chicken feed, guns, shit like that, and yet those poor old boys with nothing, go home empty-handed. Mother Luck really turned up her ass in all of our faces tonight, huh, boys?"

I really can't argue much with that, but I figure everyone goes in there with the same set of odds, so some will win, and some will lose. I sure as hell don't say that out loud, though, as Ed Jr. obviously isn't very happy about how things have worked out. I really don't think he is all that upset about Ed Sr. winning that money, but I think he's very upset at the thought of a lot of those old boys having to go home and face an empty Christmas. That's really bad, and as I sit here talkin' I can't help but think about poor old Wig. That poor shit, he's just sittin' over there in his shanty with a sick grandkid and not one single pot to piss in, and he still keeps a good attitude about things. I guess no one ever promises that life will be rosy for everyone, but it has to be a shit sandwich with cheese on top of it for poor Wig.

Brother gets cold and decides to get back in the car, and I jump right in there with him. We're both pretty excited about getting some warmth, but when Ed Jr. cranks up the car he notices that we only have about a quarter of a tank of gas left, and we still have a long-ass drive ahead of us in order to get out of these woods. On account of that he switches off the car, and now all we can do for heat is to walk and move around. Brother offers to go pick up some limbs and sticks in order to start a fire, but Ed Jr. reminds us that the light, "would draw cops like a hundred dollar bill draws a preacher" so we have to forget that idea. Anyway, what it all means is that the three of us are standing around, colder than hell, in the middle of these dark-ass woods. It's a tough row to hoe being three Juliette fugitives, I guess, or at least three potential ones. To tell ya'll the truth, I don't even like thinking about that, 'cause if half the rumors I hear about being in jail are true, the best thing you can do before going in is to tie a big, fluffy pillow around your ass. I guess if you're locked up with no hope of parole that you might be willing to do anything, but I'd drink a vomit milkshake before I'd sprinkle sugar on my biscuits, if ya'll get my drift.

My thoughts about the horrors of prison subside when we hear something from off in the distance—well, make that from off in the near distance, as the sound doesn't seem to be coming from that far away. The leaves are rustling, and there's something living that's moving around out there. Odds are, it's something that's not a big deal, but in this pitch blackness, who knows? It could be a bobcat, a bear, a fox, or maybe even worse. Ed Jr. silently walks over to the car, opens the door, and takes his pistol out of the glove compartment. He then whispers to Brother and me to get inside the car and shut the door behind us. Both of us obey and do as he asks, but we do it reluctantly 'cause we feel like we ought to be out there helping him. We do let our windows down to try to make out what's going on, and to be ready just in case our dad needs help. Besides being my dad, Ed Jr. is kinda like my best friend, and Brother and I are not gonna just sit here and let something happen to him if we can help it. He can well take care of himself, but he's also our dad, so we will be keeping an eye on him just in case.

It gets quiet for just a sec, and then you can hear more leaves rustling. Ed Jr. proceeds to get into a semi-crouching position so that he's ready for whatever happens next. Brother and I both become so tense that we couldn't slide a piece of paper between our ass cheeks if a million dollars was on the line, and we're both hoping like hell that whatever this is happens to be harmless and will just go away. And now as I hear the leaves rustling yet again, I realize that whatever it is, it's coming directly towards us. Ed Jr. becomes so motionless that it's scary, and suddenly I have to piss worse than an Irishman on blood pressure medication. The sounds are like that of something running, and as they get closer and louder, we suddenly hear, *"BLAM, BLAM, BLAM!"*

Ed Jr. has fired upon whatever it is! We're all so scared that the veins in our necks are throbbing, and I've gone from needing to piss to feeling like a five foot, ten inch bladder. The quiet after the shots is so "loud" that you can almost feel it, and after the first few seconds we notice something—whatever was making the sound in those leaves—is now silent. Totally silent. A few more seconds go by, those turn into minutes, and after about five of them we all figure that whatever was out there is dead. Ed Jr. is so confident of this that he decides to take out his flashlight and try to locate whatever it was. He walks over and opens the glove compartment to the old Falcon and takes out his flashlight. This is no damn baby flashlight, let me tell you, it carries four D batteries and is longer than an anteater's head. He flicks its switch on, and a bright beam of light shoots straight out into the blackness. He flicks the beam over to the left, right, and directly in front of us, but we see nothing—absolutely nothing. He sweeps the area with the light again, and still nothing. Finally, Brother says that he saw something move just to our right, something the light just barely caught during Ed Jr.'s last sweep of the area, and so he flicks the beam over in that direction. About ten yards right in front of us lays the carcass of an old brown rabbit. From the looks of him, he's an older one, and it's obvious that he's now a very dead one. Ed Jr. stares at it for a moment, then looks over at Brother and me and says, "Mother Luck is just grinding it right in our faces tonight, isn't she boys?"

Brother and I agree, and Ed Jr. has us all swear that we will never tell anyone that we shot a poor old brown rabbit to death out here in these woods. We all agree to tell everyone else that it was a huge red fox with a case of the rabies, and that we shot him down when he got within a few yards of us. Well, at least the distance part of this lie is true, and while it was dark it could've been possible, and Ed Jr. reminds us that we don't want people to think we're tea sippers, or worse. So a big red, rabid fox it is for the three of us, no questions asked. And, strangely enough, something good does come out of this rogue rabbit's death—it comes when Ed Jr. says, "Boys, we might as well get the hell out of here. With all the shootin' and lights and all, we've blown our cover big time. If some cops are out there, they're already on their way. We may as well drive on out of here and take our chances. What do ya'll think?"

Brother and I both agree with him so fast that it makes our heads spin. Hey, we're both chilled to the bone, and I think that prison cells are heated, so right now they're looking pretty good compared with these cold-ass woods. We all proceed to pile back into the Falcon, Ed Jr. fires her up, and we start making our way back up this long, gully-ridden dirt road. The fact that we got down here at all is pretty amazing, and the fact that Ed Jr. is getting us out of here all in one piece is testimony to his expert knowledge of these woods. We're all pretty quiet as we make our way out, I guess the combination of the chicken fight, cold woods, dead rabbit, and now potential jail time are all weighing heavily upon us at this point. To tell ya'll the truth, I'd just as soon they go ahead, slap the cuffs on us, and march us all on into the slammer. At least we'd have this nightmare over with, and I don't think Mama will throw us all out of the house over something like this. I've never, ever heard of a mama divorcing her whole family all at once, and sure, anything is possible, but I think our chances of holding on with her are pretty good. At least I'm hoping they are. It'd be hard for three potential jailbirds like us to locate a new mama/wife to break in.

Ed Jr. is driving pretty damned fast now, given the condition of the road, and he soon informs us that we are getting really close to being back out on Highway 87. He tells Brother and me not to be nervous, that the cops will be really decent about this thing and first they'll take Brother and me home, and then he'll be along shortly after. This makes Brother's eyes tear up, and mine are not too far behind. Our dad is a good man, a good father, and even if he fights chickens, it doesn't mean that he should get thrown in the slammer. I mean, where is all this Christmas spirit and compassion that everyone talks so much about? Shit, the man is just trying to make things better for his family, and his reward for that is this.

I'm about to start really praying hard to God over it, when our Falcon tops a small hill and we find ourselves back out on Highway 87. We all suck in our breath over this—at least I sense that we do. As we begin looking around, things seem to be really quiet, it's very dark and still and there's not a sound to be heard. There also doesn't seem to be a car anywhere around, 'cause the three of us are damn sure looking for one. Ed Jr. is looking around the most, and when he sees that nothing is out there, he breaks into a big smile and says, "Well, boys, the coast looks pretty damn clear to me. Looks like the sun doesn't shine on the same dog's ass all the time. And hey, at least Mother Luck did let us look up her drawers once tonight."

That pretty well sums up this entire evening. So we all go home. Get out. Go in. Get into bed. Sleep. And thank God for being able to do so…

Seven

Christmas Eve is a day like no other. It's like a warm-up holiday for the really big day, Christmas, and it's the only day I know of that has tons of customs and traditions associated with it, yet everyone wants it to get over with as soon as possible. That's a tad strange, if you really think about it—liking something yet wanting it to be over with really quickly. But I guess the good Lord created hugging semi-pretty aunts and movie shorts to help us understand that feeling.

For me, today is gonna be busy. I've gotta make a quick run over to Jenny's this afternoon in order for us to exchange gifts, and then I've gotta get back here in time for dinner. On Christmas Eve we usually eat right at six pm, and then we have this little family-type traditional thing that we do. We all go into our living room right after dinner, fire up the fireplace, and then sip on coffee or eggnog together. That's pretty nice, ain't it?

There's also the slight chance that if we beg, plead, or just plain get on Mama's nerves enough that she might let us open one Christmas gift. Underline the word "might." We'll be really lucky if that happens, though, because Ed Jr. and my mom believe in opening gifts on Christmas morning only. Mama says we do that to be sure we celebrate Jesus' birthday when we're supposed to. Ed Jr. says that we open them then so that he doesn't have to listen to any pissing and moaning about us not having any gifts left to open. He adds that if anyone has a right to a peaceful Christmas, it's him, as he has to cut down and put up the tree, deal with Mama's relatives, and pay the tab for our entire Christmas. Not to mention the fact that he's a Korean veteran. You've got to admit his logic is not bad, and at least it's pretty original.

I wake up kinda late this Christmas Eve morning. The lag from the chicken fight is still kickin' in a tad, I suppose. The three of us would've liked to sleep later, given what all happened, but Mama comes in and wakes us all up. The bad thing is, none of us can complain about it because then she'd start quizzing us about what all went on last night. She's not real crazy about these chicken fights in the first place, she's even less crazy about the gambling, and let's not even talk about how she'd react to me being in the back seat of a car with a chicken fight woman. Her breath would turn to fire and her fingernails into talons, and that would be just the start of it. Anyway, the good news is that we can all get some more rest tonight as she will be tired from all this Christmas Eve stuff, and that's good news any way you slice it. I need sleep bad, and then some.

Mama wraps up my gift for Jenny, which is a nice little gold necklace with a heart on the end of it. I bought it 'cause I know Jenny likes jewelry, and I also hope it gains me some points with her, if ya'll get my drift. I think there's as much chance of Jenny spreading her legs for me as there is of Ed Jr. deciding to take up embroidery, but one can always hope. I really do love her, but God, she makes it really hard for me to do so sometimes. I can't help but think what that gold necklace would've gotten me with last night's chicken fight woman, but that's like wonderin' what would've happened if John Holmes had gone into the priesthood. I guess, in the end, women think with their heads, and we men mostly think with the one that has a tiny little eye right in the middle of it.

Well, bad odds on tulip honin' or not, I get dressed and find myself over at Jenny's house at precisely two o'clock. When I walk inside, she's wearing a nice red sweater and gray pants, which immediately makes my zipper almost pop wide open. What's even worse is that she hugs me right after I walk in. I think sorta fast and pooch my ass back just a tad so that she won't feel Mr. Woody stretchin' out like Plastic Man here in my britches. This is sorta embarrassing, it being Christmas Eve and all, and I need to get my mind out of the gutter. That normally would be very difficult for me to do, but I can't afford to play around here, so I pull the best mental weapon that I have against horniness out of my cerebral holster and use it. I think about Coach Pitts, the head coach of my football team. Coach Pitts is a great coach and a great person, and he's one hundred percent guy. Therefore, if anything will calm down my dancing dingus, it's simply thinking about Coach Pitts.

I proceed to do just that and let nature take its course. Hey, you do what you have to sometimes. And I know that this might not be the biggest compliment that Coach Pitts has ever received, but it really is sort of a compliment to him if you think about it from a male's perspective. Whatever the case, the best news is that my trouser dirigible is shrinking, I'm starting to relax a bit and not feel like I'm carrying a toilet paper core around with me in the crotch of my britches.

After the hug, I pull my ass back in and Jenny and I wander over to the sofa and smooch for awhile. After one particularly memorable smooch, she tells me that she has a gift for me, and then proceeds to produce a white box with a huge bow on top of it. She quickly hands it to me, and I'm a tad hesitant about opening it up too quickly, as women sometimes get pretty mad if you wrinkle up the bow or tear the wrapping paper in a way that keeps them from reusing it. Jenny urges me to just go ahead and open up the box, so I do exactly that.

Man, she couldn't have gotten me a better present—it's a box filled with Baby Ruth, Butterfinger, and Pay Day candy bars. All big favorites of mine. I guess Jenny gets tickled at my "lit up" facial expression, 'cause she starts laughing and then reminds me not to eat them all up at one time. I know that I eat a lot, but there are probably thirty or more candy bars in this box. Hell, King Kong would have to be starved in order to eat them all up at once.

I thank Jenny profusely, and then go back to lookin' at all these candy bars. It occurs to me that I might need to give Jenny her gift, so I pull out the little box and hand it over to her. Jenny opens it, and I can tell that she likes the necklace 'cause her eyes almost glaze over for a second. She then hugs me again, tells me that we'd had a good year together, and I nod in complete and total agreement. Then, we sort of just stay close to each other for the rest of my visit. It's funny, we don't say very much, but sometimes you can talk to each other without a word ever having to be said. I sort of like that, to tell ya'll the truth, but I really don't understand it worth a damn.

My time with Jenny passes by quickly, and it is soon time for me to get my ass on back to the house for dinner and a quiet Christmas Eve evening. We give each other a little smooch that is a tad naughtier than I have a right to expect, and I drive myself on back home.

When I get home and walk into the kitchen, my mom is putting dinner on the table, so she tells me to go ahead and wash up. I do, and in just a few minutes Ed Jr., Brother, my mom, and I are enjoying some great fried chicken, collards, and cornbread. I'm just thankful that salmon croquettes aren't on the menu this evening. I'd rather kiss a buzzard dead on the ass than eat them.

After stuffing ourselves out three different ways, Ed Jr. gets up from the table and tells Brother and me that we oughta all go sit in the living room. The three of us head right on in there, and Brother and I watch while Ed Jr. starts stoking the fireplace with wood. That's one real plus about living out in the middle of a forest—our ass is all wrapped up with woods and trees, so having a good supply of natural heating fuel is a given. As Ed Jr. works on filling up the fireplace, Brother and I head outside to bring in more wood. The wood he's burning in there right now is pine, and it will burn up faster than a cheap K-Mart lawnmower. We also have some dried out sweet gumwood, and even a little oak piled up outside. Brother and I pick up a couple of small logs apiece, and bring them back into the house.

The walk back into the house is a lot longer on account of toting this heavy-ass wood, and by the time we both get inside, we are hassling pretty hard. Ed Jr. turns, looks at us, laughs, and then tells us that he is going to recite an old Christmas poem for us that he'd heard many years ago. We know that it is going to be good, when he tells us to sort of listen out for Mama, and that if she happens to come into the room, mum's the word. Once we all understand the ground rules, my dad clears his throat and recites this tender rhyme for us:

"Santa's outfit is red and white,
It's all that he has, but it fits just right,
His boots are black, his balls are blue,
Being cold all night does that to you.

He has a doll for Cindy,
A dog for Fred,
And a New Orleans woman,
Sittin' in his sled.

He laughs so jolly,
Never sad nor whiny,
Now he's off in his sleigh,
To hone some Louisiana heiny."

God, I bust out laughing, and Brother does the same. Ed Jr. is smiling to beat the band, but I think he gets sort of worried about Mama and tells us both to calm down a little. We reluctantly do, and the three of us are getting pretty close to breaking out a deck of cards and sneaking in a hand or two of poker when we hear some noises comin' from out in the kitchen. Before we can even get up from the fireplace to see what it is, the living room door opens, and in walks Ed Sr.

We all get somewhat quiet for a second, as we are just a tad surprised to see him here on Christmas Eve. We see him almost every day, of course, but I can never remember him showing up at our house on Christmas Eve. We've seen him before on Christmas Day, but most of the time we see him right after Christmas, as on Christmas Day we usually go over to Athens to see Grandpa and Sweetie. Traditions can and do change, I suppose.

One thing that you can always count on with Ed Sr. is that there's not usually any warming up regarding a conversation with him. He just launches off into one at the drop of a hat, and he lives up to form tonight by looking over at me and saying, "How are ya, boy? Are the tulips bloomin' in December for you?" I turn a few shades of red when he says that, which I think he thoroughly enjoys. He then takes a seat next to the fireplace and joins in our conversation, which starts taking a totally different direction. He talks at first about the Braves—"They suck worse than the smallest baby pig, and at least the damn pig has a good excuse for it"—then the price of Christmas gifts—"I don't mean to say anything wrong, but even the good Lord himself would be pissed off at some of these prices"—and he even talks a little about politics—"Democrats, Republicans, they'll all screw you, and the bad thing is that they don't even buy you dinner first." With lead-in subjects like that, it isn't long before Ed Jr. and Ed Sr. are swapping jokes back and forth, jokes that are bawdy, naughty, and whispered low so that Mama won't hear them out in the kitchen. We even position Brother close to the door so that if Mama is coming we could hear her before she enters the room.

Ed Jr. is beginning to tell a story about a mouse walking into a bar and hooking up with a female giraffe when my brother says that he can hear someone pulling up in our driveway. I go over and pull open the curtain to our big living room window, and sure enough, you could see headlights from a car pulling up. The only problem is that it's so dark that you can't really make out anything about the car. You can tell that it's moving really slowly, but, after all, it is coming up a driveway. Ed Jr., Ed Sr., and I quickly decide to walk outside to find out just who in the hell this might be.

The three of us quickly get out of the house, walk

outside, and immediately find ourselves blinded. The car that's just pulled up is stopped about fifteen feet or so away, and they're just sitting there with their bright lights on and their engine idling. The lights are so bright that you can't see anything, and finally Ed Sr. hollers out, "Dammit to hell, turn down those bright-ass lights! Do you think that the three of us want our eyes dilated right here on Christmas Eve?"

I am worried right after he says that, as we don't have a clue just who might be in that car, but this particular mystery ends very quickly for the three of us. Just as soon as those words get out of Ed Sr.'s mouth, the car's lights dim, its engine stops, and I see old Wig getting out of his battered Chevy Impala. That seeing him tonight is a surprise goes without saying. Honestly, I figure he must be looking for a Christmas Eve hand-out, and Ed Sr. is undoubtedly thinking the same thing because he looks right at Wig and asks, "Wig, what do you want? You haven't come here lookin' for money have you, 'cause if you have, I'm not giving you one thin dime!"

Old Wig nods politely, and then replies, "Mistah Ed, I have come to give you dese." And with that, he reaches over into his car, pulls out the set of jumper cables that Ed Sr. loaned him back on Thanksgiving Day, and places them back in his hands.

It's funny, I've never seen Ed Sr. when he didn't have something to say to somebody, but he suddenly seems very lost for words. Ed Jr. is the very same way, it's like both of them have suddenly lost their ability to communicate.

Wig, however, has more to say, so he does, "I figured I's needed to give dis back to you, Mistah Ed, after the good fortune that my sistah Louisa Mae found. Even though she and her chirrens is po and needed food, medicine, and work done on her car, someone slipped an envelope in her mailbox dat had over five hundred dollars in it, Mr. Ed! Five hundred dollars! Louisa Mae and her chirrens just about shit in dey pants, dey felt so good! Dat money will buy dem some medicine for sick little Chantice, turn dey lights back on, fix de car, and will buy a nice Christmas present for each child. It is a blessing from

God fo sure, Mr. Ed! When I saw and heard all dat, I had to bring back dese jumper cables, 'cause you might be able to help someone else who be in trouble and be in need one day when dey is out driving. They have already hepped me more than I can say."

I don't know what to say. Hell, none of us do. I look over at Ed Jr. and he is looking at his father with an expression that I've never seen before.

Old Wig continues, "Mistah Ed, the baby Jesus has spread His good will all over my family, and old Santy Claus will carry a big ole bag across de sky tonight. I just want you and both of the other Mistah Eds here to know how grateful I is, and not to worry about ole Wig. God has took real good care of me."He then shakes all of our hands, gets in his car, and drives off.

Not a one of us say a word—not Ed Sr., Ed Jr., or myself. I don't know whether to smile or cry, and I'm now seeing both my dad and granddad in a very different light. For all of his gruffness and cussin' and stuff, Ed Sr. has a very tender heart, and can show Christian charity towards those less fortunate than he. He's just helped me understand what Christmas is truly supposed to be about. About the only other thing I can tell ya'll here is that the three of us do a little more quiet thinkin', gather ourselves, and then go back inside, very thankful that the baby Jesus had made His way to this earth and set an example for all of us to live by. An example that I've just witnessed firsthand, right out here in our driveway…

Eight

I wish that I could tell ya'll that some other really good things happen this Christmas, but they don't. Ed Sr. went back to his house right after Wig left, and my family and I sit up a while longer, then call it a night. I do think about Wig a little more tonight, though, and what he had done. God really can touch your heart, and I do believe that He does things sometimes just to let you know that He's there. It's the last thing that I think this Christmas Eve, as I drop off to sleep right after thinking it.

I should end this story here, but I guess I do need to throw in one more thing. About two o'clock this morning I hear a heavy clumping sound go by my window—I kid ya'll not, a heavy clumping sound. Once I shake myself awake, I swear that I hear the same sound again a couple of minutes later, and along with it I hear what sounds like a person running. It startles me so much that I get up and walk into Ed Jr.'s room just to let him know about it. When I go in there, I discover he isn't in his bed. The sheets and blankets are pushed back like he's just gotten up.

I figure I'd better go check things out, so I walk through the house and out into the garage, and then I tiptoe over to the edge of the garage so that I can look out into our yard. I see nothing right at first, but in about twenty seconds a white-looking blur clumps around the side of the house, and I realize that it's R. L. Watkins' pony, and he's on the loose again. He's running like a panther with his ass on fire, and the reason why appears soon enough—it's Ed Jr., and he's right behind him, running like a possessed man with a rifle in his hands. R. L.'s pony knows that he'd better get the hell out of our yard, and he makes it halfway down the driveway when Ed Jr. raises his weapon, pulls the trigger, and *"BLAMMMM!"* I hear the shot make solid contact with the pony's ass, you really can hear the buckshot hitting it, and the pony makes this really loud, *"WHINNNNNNNNNNN"* sound and double-times it out of our driveway and on down the road.

At this point Ed Jr. takes a few deep breaths, looks over at me, and says, "That sonofabitch got loose again, and brought his ass right on up here to my house. What the attraction here is for the bastard I don't know, he can eat grass anywhere, but he has to bring his sorry ass up here and eat mine. This time, I figured that he needed to be sent a damned message that he won't soon forget. I should've gone on ahead and put him out of his misery, but I just popped him in the ass because it's Christmas, dammit. I respect the holiday, because that's the kind of God-fearing man I am. If it weren't for that, I'd have sent his good-for-glue ass straight to that big Elmer's factory up in the sky!"

It's Christmas, indeed…

About Ed

Ed Williams is a true Southern Outlaw Author who hails from Juliette, Georgia. He's the author of the books *Sex, Dead Dogs, and Me: The Juliette Journals*, and *Rough As A Cob: More From The Juliette Journals.* A recent story, *Sally the Screamer,* appeared in the Southern humor anthology, *Southern Fried Farce.* He also loves ICEEs, Bachman-Turner Overdrive, Atomic Fireballs, and anyone who appreciates honin' a good tulip.

5846706R0

Made in the USA
Lexington, KY
20 June 2010